JAYLA WHITE DAVIS
LOVE
Lifted
ME
The Novel

For permission requests, contact: Seed Life Publishing
www.seedlifenetwork.com

Cover design by Jayla White Davis
ISBN: 979-8-9987505-0-2
Printed in the United States of America First Edition

Published by Seed Life Publishing
Jackson, Georgia

To my Beloved Late Grandma Annie Gail Bell,

The woman who taught me to write and encouraged me to tell my stories. Your wisdom and love have shaped me in ways words can't fully express.

And to the Lord,

Who is the head of my life, may You receive all the glory. For without You, none of this would be possible.

Dear Reader,

First and foremost, thank you. Thank you for choosing this book, for welcoming these characters into your heart, and for allowing me to share a piece of my heart with you. *Love Lifted Me* was born out of a desire to tell the truth, not just about relationships, but about redemption, healing, and the kind of love that truly transforms.

This story began as a live stage play performance filled with emotion, but I always knew it had more to say. Turning it into a novel gave the characters space to breathe, to struggle, and to grow in a way that I hope resonates deeply within you.

If you've ever experienced heartbreak, felt unseen, or questioned your worth, this story is for you. If you've ever doubted whether true, God - anchored love can still transform lives, I pray this book serves as a reminder.

My goal isn't just to entertain, but to point hearts back to the One who restores all things. Whether you're in a waiting season, a rebuilding season, or a walking-away season, I hope this story meets you right where you are.

Thank you for being on this journey with me. I don't take it lightly. Keep daring to love. Keep daring to create. Above all, keep giving God the glory.

With all my heart,
Jayla White Davis

LOVE LIFTED ME

JAYLA WHITE DAVIS

Chapter 1
Shake Up

When I started building my life in the fashion industry, I thought I was doing the right thing. I never had it easy. No mom, no dad just me, my brother, and our grandmother. My brother chose the path of prison, and I chose mine.

I met my fine, handsome husband back in high school, and we've been together ever since. We've weathered some storms, and when things got hard, I did what I had to do for the both of us. I've climbed my way up in fashion industry from nothing. Now people are literally begging to work with me. I've styled the best of the best, and I don't take that for granted.

But it does get lonely sometimes.

I've made good friends out here in New York, but I still miss my husband… my brother… my friends back home. Chasing this dream meant choosing money over comfort. Carter was hurt physically, mentally from losing his dad and a sports injury. He went into a dark, depressed place. So, I picked up our life and ran with it. Somebody had to. I wasn't about to end up like my mama, letting drugs swallow her whole and left us with nothing.

Sometimes I feel like everyone wants me to be something I'm not. Always the strong one. Always smiling. This decision I'm making now. It's not for them.

It's for me.

Mya pressed her lipstick to her lips, carefully tracing the familiar curve of her mouth. She gave herself one final look in the mirror, tilting her head slightly, as if searching for something beyond her reflection. With a steadying breath, she stood up and walked across the room towards her phone. Her fingers hovered for just a second before tapping the screen to call her husband.

No answer.

She stared at the phone for a moment longer, as if willing it to ring.

A soft knock interrupted her thoughts.

Knock knock.

"Everything alright in there?" Chase's voice came from the other side of the door, gentle but curious.

Mya blinked, then looked away from her phone, doing her best to let go of the weight sitting on her chest.

"Yes, everything is alright," she called back, her voice calm and composed.

She stepped into the bathroom, flicked on the light, and looked into the mirror. Her eyes met her own, and she took a deep breath.

"I am strong. I am loved. I am enough," she whispered, affirming the truth she needed to hear.

A small, almost imperceptible smile tugged at her lips.

Back At Home

"Will we ever be able to go back mom?" Olivia's voice trembled, the weight of uncertainty pressing down on her.

James turned to her, his tone blunt and protective. "For what? She didn't give us anything but pain."

The night was thick with tension as young James and Olivia walked through the dimly lit streets of the neighborhood.

"You two, keep up. It's already late," Andrea's voice cut through the stillness, sharp and commanding.

Sirens wailed, further disturbing the fragile peace of the night.

Olivia's lip quivered. "James, that's our mom. What are they going to do to her?"

James' jaw clenched. He looked ahead, trying to push the thoughts of their mother out of his mind, knowing he had to be strong. "Get her some help," he said, trying to sound convincing. "Try something new for once."

As the night stretched on, the sound of distant gunshots echoed briefly before silence once again consumed the world around them.

James and Olivia flinched at the noise, instinctively ducking for cover. Andrea's eyes darted around, ever vigilant, guiding them forward.

Ray Ray came running, his footsteps heavy, his breathing ragged, followed by Tina, who stormed after him, fury in her eyes.

"Ray Ray! I know dang well you weren't coming out of that woman's house!" Tina's voice was sharp.

Ray Ray held his hands up in defense, "Tina will you chill. That's not what I was doing" he pleaded, but Tina wasn't having it.

"Yeah yeah, I bet you wasn't" Tina said, taking a step toward him. "And I'm gonna make sure you won't ever again."

Ray Ray, desperate now, took a step back. "Hold on, Tina! Calm down!" he begged, but before he could say more, the crack of a gunshot rang out.

The air thickened with the sound of a single, terrifying gunshot. The street fell into an eerie hush, the moment hanging suspended in time. Tina stood still for a heartbeat; her eyes widened as she looked at the gun in her hand.

"Now I know you won't do it again," she muttered, her voice cold and final. Ray Ray slid away, disappearing, and Tina watched after him, satisfaction flickering across her face.

Tina's breath came in sharp, uneven bursts as she paced back to the apartment. "I'm so tired of him cheating on me..." Her words hung heavy in the air, raw and desperate. She sniffled, wiping her eyes, but the tears wouldn't fall not yet. Her anger was the only thing that felt real, the only thing she could hold on to.

She wiped her palms on her jeans, the rough fabric grounding her, but her mind wouldn't stop spinning. Memories of Ray Ray—the lies, the promises, the broken trust—flashed through her mind like a relentless slideshow. He was supposed to be her rock. He was supposed to love her.

Her phone buzzed in her hand, dragging her back to the present. The screen lit up with a message from Mya: "You're invited to the grand opening of my new boutique! Come celebrate with me!"

Tina paused mid-step, the words glowing up at her. For a moment, she didn't move. Mya? She hadn't seen her best friend in ages. The one who ran as soon as she saw her dreams coming to life.

Tina sat down on the couch, the invitation still glowing in her hand. Her finger hovered over the screen. She felt a small tug at her heart as she stared at Mya's message: the grand opening invitation to her boutique.

Tina just went ahead and clicked Yes. I'll go. She quickly texted Diana: Girl you got the invite? You going?

She walked to the kitchen, grabbed herself a coke, and sipped it down. She grabbed her bonnet from the counter and pulled it over her head.

Meanwhile, Mya stood backstage at her latest New York fashion show, her heart heavy despite the flurry of excitement around her. The lights of the runway sparkled, and the buzz of the crowd was electric. Her designs were praised, her models were dazzling, and yet, none of it mattered. Her thoughts were elsewhere.

Mya looked up and saw London approaching her, her assistant of two years. London was sharp, business-minded, and always there when Mya needed her.

Mya turned to London with a grin, trying to hide the undercurrent of worry gnawing at her. "So, I see the invitations went out?" she said, her voice light.

London smiled; her eyes bright as she adjusted the hem of her dress. "They sure did. Everything is under control Mya." Mya nodded, though she wasn't so sure anymore. She had her life all mapped out she was successful, admired, powerful, but the cracks were starting to show, the loneliness creeping in when no one was around. She had tried reaching out to Carter all day, but he hadn't responded to any of her calls or texts.

Just then, one of Mya's major sponsors, a sleek and confident woman in a tailored suit, approached her. She took Mya's hand, her voice soothing yet filled with business intent.

"You did an amazing job tonight, Mya. This show was everything. You've outdone yourself."

Mya smiled at the compliment, but her eyes scanned the crowd. "Thank you. But I—" she started to say, but her words were interrupted as the woman continued to speak.

"Do you have to leave so soon? I mean, the after-party is just getting started. We need to talk more about your future projects. The world is yours, Mya. Don't waste it."

Mya forced a smile. "I'll be right back," she lied. She excused herself and made her way toward the bar, where Chase was waiting.

Chase, her friend and business partner from college, gave her a knowing look. "Everything okay, Mya?" His voice was filled with genuine concern, and for a moment, Mya wanted to spill everything—the emptiness she couldn't shake, the cracks in her marriage, the nagging feeling that maybe she was missing out on something more.

Instead, she smiled, the smile she had perfected over the years—the one that hid everything. "Yeah, everything's fine what you over here at the bar doing?" she said, changing the subject.

Chase took a sip of his water, let out a soft laugh, and said, "Just needed a quick step away. I never thought we'd be here."

Mya gave a subtle smile. "I didn't either, but…I'm glad we are."

Chase glanced around, his eyes panning across the room full of people laughing and dancing at the afterparty. Then he turned to her.

"You sure about that?"

Mya tilted her head, caught off guard. "Yeah. Why you ask?"

"Well," Chase said, his tone shifting as his gaze locked on hers, "you're leaving here tomorrow."

Mya's eyes widened. "What?"

He tilted his head. "I know everything Mya, you don't have to hide it."

She paused, then nodded back. "I'm just going to the next chapter of my life."

Chase's brow furrowed. "And that means leaving everything you built?"

"I'm not leaving it," she said quietly. "I'm adding to it."

He nodded again, but this time there was a certain weight in his expression. "Well…I hope you're enjoying your night, Mya. You built all of this. You deserve it."

She smiled, but just barely. Behind the smile was a swirl of guilt she didn't want anyone to see. The truth was, she didn't feel like she deserved it. Not fully. Not with the way she was leaving everything and everyone behind.

Chase gave her a soft tap on the shoulder and walked away.

Mya stood in place for a moment, her chest tight. Then she turned to the bar.

"Cranberry juice, please," she said.

As the bartender slid the glass toward her, she picked it up, took a slow sip, and turned to make her way toward London.

Slipping into the noise of the after-party doing her best not to be seen. The music was loud, the crowd was dancing to the familiar rhythms of the Cha-Cha Slide, and of course, the Wobble. She couldn't help but chuckle as she watched the guests move in sync, the joy of the dance filling the air. For a moment, it was easy to pretend everything was fine.

Later, after the party had wound down, Mya found herself sitting alone on a plush couch, the music and laughter fading into the background.

Chapter 2
The Move

The sound of movers pulling into the driveway broke through the quietness of the early morning. Mya hadn't gotten much sleep. Her mind had been racing all night—thoughts bouncing between excitement and guilt, clarity and doubt. Regardless of how she felt, she was ready for this. Still in her oversized tee and socks, Mya stepped out of her room and headed downstairs. The movers were already at work, hauling boxes out the door with practiced ease. Her things were carefully labeled and stacked were disappearing, one by one.

She had decided to leave the furniture behind. Even though she was moving back home, she wasn't ready to let go of the house. Not yet. Maybe not ever. In the kitchen, she brewed a fresh pot of coffee, the familiar smell bringing her a small sense of calm. Once it was ready, she poured herself a cup, added cream and a little sweetener, then cradled it in her hands.

With a quiet sigh, she walked into the living room and sat down on the couch. She took a sip and watched as the last pieces of her life here were carried away. The mansion her symbol of success, felt smaller now. Not in the literal sense, but in the emotional sense. The life she had built in New York, the empire she had crafted, was now scattered in the backs of trucks. Next thing you know Chase walked in.

"So, this is it, huh?" His voice was calm.

Mya paused, her lips pressed together in a thin line.

"I hate to say it, but looks like it" she said, her voice soft while folding her arms.

Chase stood there, frozen for a moment, clearly taken aback. His eyes searched hers, his expression flickering with a mix of disbelief and pain. "I will handle everything while you go handle the south."

Mya's throat tightened as she looked around the vast, empty space, the walls now hollow. "Sometimes you have to make changes, right," she said, her voice shaking slightly. "Sometimes you have to choose what matters most." She looked at him.

Chase nodded. There was nothing left for him to say.

"Thank you for everything, Chase," Mya said, her voice gentle now, as though she were speaking to him for the last time. "I love you. Seriously, you've been there for me in ways that no one else ever has. I'll never forget that."

"Why are you talking like we aren't ever going to do anything again? Your life isn't over." Chase said.

Chase wanted to say so much more, to tell her how he felt, how he had loved her from the moment they met, but the words didn't come out for one she is married. Instead, he just nodded.

She turned away, walking toward the door, and with one last look over her shoulder, she was gone.

Chase stood frozen on the front steps of the now empty house, as she disappeared into the distance.

The Uber was quiet as Mya sat in the back, staring out the side window. The city she had called home for the last few years was fading behind her, and the familiar sights of her old country town were slowly coming into view.

They turned down the road that led to her boutique—the new place she had poured everything into. Mya glanced out at the modest storefront. She put on her sunglasses, as if to shield herself from the weight of what she was doing. She took a deep breath, trying to steady herself. I'm doing this, she thought. *I'm really doing this.*

With a sharp nod to the driver, she spoke firmly, "Wait for me." The words felt solid final.

She turned towards the door of her boutique. Her heart heavy, yet resolute.The thought of her husband, Carter, kept her grounded.

I did this for him, she reminded herself. I chose this. I chose him.

She had tried to ignore the fact that their marriage was crumbling, that they were drifting further and further apart. So, here she was sacrificing everything she had worked for, everything that was hers, for a chance to rebuild with him. She didn't even know if it would work, but she had to try.

She closed her eyes and let out a long, slow breath. *Sometimes you must sacrifice. Sometimes you must give up what you love the most to get what you need.*

The boutique was alive with the smells of fresh polished wood, and a soft flowery scent.

London, her assistant and somewhat a friend, moved around the store, organizing the clothes with practiced precision. Mya knew London took a massive risk by stepping away from her rising career in the fashion industry, leaving behind the glitz of New York Fashion Week to open this boutique.

"Everything finally coming together. I did the best I could" London grinned, stepping back to admire her work.

Mya laughed, shaking her head. “It looks amazing, you definitely made something out of nothing.”

London raised an eyebrow. “I had to make something happen. I can’t believe we skipped the rest of New York Fashion Week just to open your clothing store in the hood.”

Mya laughed softly, “This is bigger than New York Fashion Week I promise this will be worth it and this is not the hood. This is home.”

London let out a short laugh, I heard a girl named Tina just shot her baby daddy for talking to his other baby mama.”

Mya chuckled, trying to hide the tension creeping up her spine. “Hold up that’s my best friend. I can’t believe they are still at it. Well, it might not be the best, but it’s still home.”

The door swung open, and Trevor strolled in, a grin plastered on his face.

“Ayo, sis! They said you were here I didn’t believe it” Trevor greeted loudly, drawing Mya's attention.

Mya's face lit up when she saw him. “OMG Trevor !?”

Trevor tossed a small package in the air, catching it effortlessly. “Here. this package came for you in the mail. I see this place is coming along.”

Mya stepped closer, excitement bubbling in her chest. “Thank you! So, what do you think?”

He glanced around, his eyes narrowing. “I mean, you’ve definitely turned it around in here. Nothing I can wear, but it’s nice for women.”

Mya laughed, rolling her eyes. “You’ve always been my biggest hater.”

Trevor raised his hands in mock defense. "Nah, nah, sis never that."

Mya let out an exasperated sigh. "Go away, Trevor. We don't need none of that bad energy. London, go get the sage."

Trevor burst out laughing. "The sage? You turned to that ooga booga stuff I know big Mama turning in her grave."

Mya smiled knowingly. "Big Mama has her ways, and I have mine."

Trevor shook his head with a grin. "I hear you. Well, let me get to this interview, Miss Sage."

The door swung open, and in walked Diana. The moment Mya saw her, her face broke into a wide smile, and they embraced for a moment, the familiar comfort of their friendship washing over Mya.

Diana pulled back after a second, holding Mya at arm's length and taking in the space. "Hold up," she said, eyes wide in disbelief. "I must be dreaming right now. Look at this place!"

Mya laughed, her heart lightening at the sight of her best friend. "Girl, you're not dreaming. This is all real."

Diana's eyes swept the boutique, inspecting every inch of it. "Mya, this is beautiful! The outside and inside look completely different. You've really done it."

Mya grinned, feeling the pride swell in her chest again. "Thank you. You know how long I've wanted this."

Diana leaned in closer, her voice dropping to a more serious tone. "You have cameras and a safe, right?"

Mya slapped her playfully on the shoulder, chuckling. "Girl, you are a mess. Of course."

Diana raised an eyebrow, not convinced. "Okay, okay but seriously, this place looks amazing. I can't wait to see how you turn this into a success, like you do everything else."

Mya's smile softened, the weight of her efforts making her voice a little more reflective. "Girl, we are living our dreams. You're a wonderful lawyer, and I'm a fashion designer."

Diana grinned, nodding. "Yes, girl, yes! To God be all the glory."

Mya shook her head playfully, giving a small laugh. "No, to us. All the glory to us."

Diana laughed, though her face turned thoughtful. "I'm going to give God my glory but put me to work I'm here to help."

London, who had been organizing nearby, jumped in quickly. "You sure can! I need help with these boxes."

The bell above the door chimed as the Uber driver walked back into the boutique, his expression a little less than friendly. He glanced around the room before locking eyes with Mya.

"Did you forget about me?" he asked, his tone flat.

Diana and London both stopped what they were doing, surprised by his tone. Mya, still moving around behind the counter, froze for a moment and then quickly covered her mouth in embarrassment.

"Oh my God, I did," she exclaimed. "I'm so sorry!" She rushed over to him, pulling out cash from her purse. "Here, I can pay you. I really appreciate you waiting."

The driver took the money without much enthusiasm, shaking his head.

London, who had been watching the exchange, made a face. "Rude. He could've at least said thank you." The bell above the door rang.

Carter stepped into the boutique, his tall frame filling the doorway. Mya couldn't hide the joy on her face as she quickly made her way toward him. "Hey babe! I was headed home" she said, her voice light, hopeful.

Carter didn't return her enthusiasm. His face was distant, his eyes cold as he stood there, taking in the space. "Hey, Mya," he replied, his tone flat, like something was off. He glanced around, looking over the store with a critical eye.

Mya, sensing the tension, immediately looked around to make sure no one else was listening. Her concern was written all over her face. She moved a little closer to him, lowering her voice. "You okay, Carter? What's going on?"

He stepped back, his jaw tightening. His voice was sharp, colder now. "Yeah, this came to the house for you." He paused, eyeing her intensely.

This wasn't the reunion she had imagined. She studied his face, searching for any sign of the man she had married—the man she was still trying to hold on to. Slowly, she replied, her voice trembling a little. "Thank you, are you sure everything is, okay? Are you not happy to see me?"

His face remained unchanged. "This is just so sudden." He crossed his arms. "You didn't think to discuss any of this with me first?"

Mya's heart twisted. She glanced down at the floor, frustration bubbling up. "Well, if you would check your phone," she said quietly, "you would see I've been calling you and leaving messages. You haven't answered any of them."

Before Carter could reply, Diana, who had been standing off to the side, stepped forward with a bright smile, trying to break the tension. "Hey Carter," she said, her voice warm, "what do you think about this place? It looks amazing, doesn't it? I know you're proud of Mya."

Carter's eyes flickered toward Diana, He made a face, clearly not impressed. "She started a store in the hood. Nothing really to be proud of." He turned his back to them, heading for the door. "I'll see you at the house, Mya," he said curtly as he left, the door slamming behind him.

Mya stood there trying to hold it together, but it was so hard. She glanced at Diana, who watched her with concern. Mya trying not to draw any attention to what just happened.

Diana, sensing her friend's pain. "Girl what's up with him? Are you and Carter, okay?" Her voice was soft, full of care.

Before Mya could respond, the door swung open again, and in walked Tina, her loud, vibrant energy filling the room. She paused for a moment, looking around in awe.

"Girrrl!" Tina's voice boomed. "This place is nice! No roaches or nothing, huh? Wow, girl, you've really done it." She couldn't stop smiling as she looked around, clearly impressed.

Mya's eyes lit up when she saw Tina ready to change the subject. She walked over quickly and pulled her into a tight hug. "Tina, girl, it is so good to see you! It's been forever!"

Tina laughed and hugged her back, pulling away with a big grin. "Girl, it really has been. How are you? How's everything?"

Mya smiled but couldn't help feeling the weight of everything that had just happened. "I'm good. How about you?"

Tina gave a dramatic, almost theatrical laugh, her voice turning a little fake. "Girl, I'm holding in there, you know?"

Diana, who had been quietly watching from the side, now moved forward to hug Tina. "Look at us, back together again," she said, her voice full of warmth.

Tina grinned, pulling back to look at all of them. "I know, right? All my girls in one spot. It feels good."

Chapter 3
Unbearable

Mya walked around the boutique, making sure everything was in place before she left for the evening. The store wasn't officially open yet, but she had spent most of the day prepping, fixing minor details.

The door swung open, and the familiar, booming voices of Pastor Wallace and First Lady Sabrina filled the room.

"Hallelujah! Glory be to God! This is beautiful! God is so good!" First Lady Sabrina's high-pitched voice echoed through the space as she stepped in with Pastor Wallace right behind her, both of them practically glowing with energy and praise.

Mya's face shifted slightly, irritated. She quickly walked over, a polite but strained smile on her face. "Uh, I'm not open yet," she said softly, trying to keep things friendly.

However, before she could say more, Diana, who had been in the back room, walked out and smiled brightly at the sight of the visitors. "Oh, they're here for me!" Diana exclaimed, walking toward First Lady Sabrina and Pastor Wallace with an open arms gesture. "How are you both doing?"

First Lady Sabrina practically beamed as she embraced Diana. "We're blessed, darling! So blessed! This place... it's just incredible!" She took a slow look around the boutique, her fingers grazing the fabric of a dress on display. "God really has a way of showing up, doesn't He?"

Diana smiled, already engaging with the First Lady. "Oh, yes, He does. You know, this is my friend Mya place."

First Lady Sabrina's eyes lit up with recognition. She turned to Mya, her expression shifting from admiration to something softer, almost nostalgic. "Mya? Oh, baby, I remember your grandmother. She was a powerful woman of prayer, an intercessor. She held that whole church together in ways most people don't know about."

Mya's expression tightened, her lips pressing into a thin line as she heard the mention of her grandmother. She looked away "She gave more to that church than she ever gave to her own family," Mya said.

Diana, caught off guard by Mya's coldness, took a halfstep back, but the First Lady didn't seem to acknowledge it. Then she answered and said "Well, she enjoyed every minute of it."

Mya, no longer wanted to have this conversation. She turned on her heel and walked off, heading to the back of the store. "I need a minute," she called over her shoulder, her tone clipped.

Diana watched her leave, a slight frown on her face. "I'm sorry about that," she said apologetically to the First Lady. "She's going through something right now."

First Lady raised an eyebrow but remained graceful. "Oh, baby, just because I'm saved doesn't mean I don't understand that people go through things. Life is tough, but God's got us and I'm still from the hood I can handle it."

Just as Diana was about to respond, First Lady Sabrina's tone became more businesslike. "Speaking of tough things, darling, I need your help. I'm working on getting everything together for the church ball, and I need you to help me with it" Sabrina asked with a glimmer in her eye.

Diana hesitated. "Well, Mya is a designer and I'm pretty sure she would love to help."

The First Lady didn't miss a beat. She was already clapping her hands in delight. "Perfect! I know Mya's talented, and she always had her grandma looking good."

Pastor Wallace, who had been silently observing the exchange, nodded and said, "Alright, Sabrina, we gotta get up out of this hood." He moved toward the door.

First Lady Sabrina eagerly followed him, her enthusiasm barely contained. "We'll talk soon, Diana! Don't forget now!"

As the door swung closed behind them, Tina walked over to Diana and leaned in close and whispered, "Girl, you know Mya's about to get you for that one."

Diana shrugged nonchalantly, unfazed. "No, she won't hush." Her voice was light, but the edge of guilt in her tone was hard to miss.

Mya walked back in at that exact moment.

Tina wasted no time, her words blunt as always. "That girl," she pointed at Diana, "just offered you to do First Lady's dress for the church ball."

Mya froze. "No, no, no. Why 'D'? Why would you do that?" she asked, her tone frustrated, her arms crossed over her chest.

Diana, slightly caught off guard by Mya's reaction, took a deep breath. "I'm sorry, Mya. They need help it's for the church"

Mya shook her head, cutting her off. "I have enough going on already, Diana. I can't take on any more definitely not all that glory glory mess today!" She turned away, grabbing her purse from the counter.

Diana stepped forward; her eyes wide, "Mya, wait—"

Before she could say anything else, the door opened again. A woman walked in, her professional demeanor immediately evident.

"Are you Mya?" the woman asked, her tone businesslike.

Mya sighed, her frustration rising. She turned to the woman. "Yes, I'm Mya. How can I help you?"

The woman introduced herself as a social worker. "I'm here to talk to you about adoption," she said, her words formal.

Mya's heart dropped, but she kept her composure. "Yes, let's talk over here" she said softly.

Mya leads her over to the register. The social worker then asked a crucial question. "Adoption is a wonderful thing, I see that you are married, but I don't see your husband signature, have you spoken to your husband about this decision?"

Mya hesitated. She shook her head slowly. "No," she whispered, her voice almost inaudible. "Not yet it's a surprise."

"This is a huge step, and we need both of you to be in one accord before moving forward. I will come by later for you both to sign the documents." The social worker exclaimed.

Mya not knowing what to do, she just nods. The social worker walks out of the boutique.

The others in the room heard everything, and the air seemed to thicken with the unspoken tension. Tina was the first to speak. "Girl, a surprise!" she laughed harshly. "He's not gonna like that one bit. You know how that man is."

Mya looked up at Tina, confused. "What are you talking about?"

Tina smirked. "Girl, you know what I mean. Carter is set in his ways. You think he's going to be okay with you bringing in a child that's not his? Please."

Mya's face hardened. "I'm not about to listen to this," she snapped. "I need to go home."

Diana stepped in quickly, looking at tina. "Hush, Tina. You're all in Mya's business. Let her handle it her way."

Mya, feeling overwhelmed and frustrated, grabbed her things and made for the door.

Tina, looking around to make sure Mya was really gone, leaned back against the wall and let out a sharp breath. "I can't believe that girl is planning on adopting and not telling Carter" she said, shaking her head. "Girl, she stays doing sneaky stuff."

Diana exhaled slowly, "I know right I can't wrap my head around it. Why wouldn't she talk to Carter first?"

Tina nodded, crossing her arms. "It's like she's always got these unrealistic views about Carter. Like she's putting up this perfect front, but we all see the cracks."

London, who had been quietly listening, stepped over to where they stood, her brows furrowed. "Do y'all think It's right to be talking about her in her store?" she asked, raising an eyebrow.

Diana sighed, her shoulders slumping slightly. "We're not talking about her. We're just… trying to figure out how we can support her. It's just hard, you know? She's always making these decisions that don't make any sense."

Tina shook her head again. "Girl, she's always been that way since high school." London turned toward Diana with an inquisitive look. "Wait—hold up. How long has she been married? Because Carter never shows up to any of her events.

Even while she was doing all that work in New York, he was nowhere to be found."

Diana's eyes and she glanced at Tina both of them exchanged a knowing look. They both had been aware of the absence of Carter in Mya's life, but they didn't know it was that bad.

"What do you mean, he's never there?" Tina burst out, her voice loud with disbelief.

"I've never met him. I've heard Mya talk about him, yeah, but I've never seen him a day in my life" London says. Her expression shifted from confusion to suspicion, as if the pieces of a puzzle were starting to fall into place.

Tina folded her arms tightly across her chest. "This just doesn't feel right. Carter probably still don't have a job," she added, her voice laced with disbelief.

"Tina!" Diana said, raising her voice in warning.

Tina held up her hands in mock surrender, but the sharpness in her voice didn't falter. "I'm just saying, it's time we call a spade a spade. She's been taking care of him since high school, and now he's got the nerve to not support her. That's what we need to be talking about."

Diana's face twisted into a concerned frown. "But it's Mya we're talking about. She doesn't see it that way. She sees the good in him. She's holding on to something, hoping it'll work out, even when we all see what's really happening." She turned to London. "What do you think?"

London shook her head slowly, "I don't know. I just think that woman is holding way too much in. I don't know too much of this side of her. All I know is she is the top of the top who wanted to come home to all of you guys."

Tina exhaled dramatically, running a hand through her hair. "I can't be caught up in this she wants to act like she got it I'm going to let her. So, this isn't none of our business" she said, pushing off the wall. She turned to Diana, her eyes narrow. "It was good meeting you, London, but I'm outta here."

"Well, all I can do is pray for her," Diana said softly. "I need to get home—are you going to be alright here by yourself?"

London grabbed her purse. "I'll leave out with you. I'm not familiar with the area."

Diana raised an eyebrow as London started gathering her things. "So… you're moving here too?"

London nodded, flipping off the lights in the back. "Yes, I am. Mya helped me get into the fashion world so however I can help her then I'm going to."

Diana smiled. "That's nice of you. So where are you staying?"

"I got an apartment up towards the town," London said with a smile.

Diana laughed again, her voice light. "The good part."

London grinned. "Yes, girl. I did my research."

They stepped outside together, locking up behind them.

Chapter 4
The Matter at Hand

Mya stepped out of the Uber, her feet sinking into the familiar, uneven concrete of her old neighborhood. The air was thick, hot and sticky with the kind of heat that made it hard to breathe, especially in the city where the summer never seemed to end. She paused for a moment, taking it all in. Nothing had changed.

Across the street, her grandparents' house sat in silence, the shutters still bolted up tight on the windows. Trevor, her younger brother, had been living there for years now, but he still hadn't bothered to fix the house up. It was the same run-down place she'd grown up in covered in faded paint, its windows cracked, its roof sagging. Mya's heart ached as she thought about all the times her grandparents had worked tirelessly to keep the house standing, and now Trevor had let it rot.

She shook her head, glancing down the street. The old hood was still the same too filled with older people sitting on their porches, talking about everyone and everything in the neighborhood. She couldn't help but roll her eyes. It was like nothing ever moved forward here. Just a bunch of people stuck in the past.

Then, as her eyes traveled back to her front yard, a wave of frustration hit her. Carter hadn't even bothered to bring her things inside. Her clothes, her bags, her personal belongings. All of it was scattered on the porch and even spilled into the yard. Her things were out there like they didn't matter, just waiting to be picked through by anyone passing by. Mya muttered to herself, "Wow, anybody could've gotten my stuff…"

She huffed in disbelief as she grabbed a couple of bags, dragging them up the porch steps with a groan. As soon as she stepped inside, the familiar musty smell hit her. A smell she hadn't even noticed before but now seemed impossible to ignore. The house looked exactly as it had six years ago when she left. The countertops still needed to be replaced, the old wood paneling on the walls, the worn-out furniture. The place felt like a time capsule stuck in a past that she had moved on from.

She wandered through the small house, her steps slow and heavy. Every room felt like a reminder of everything she'd tried to escape. She had dreamed of a better life, one filled with luxury and success, but here she was, back in the same old place.

The kitchen hadn't been touched. The air was thick with neglect. Her home was nothing like the mansion she had in New York.

Carter still wasn't home. He was probably doing whatever he always did since she's been gone. Mya sighed; heart heavy with the uncertainty of it all.

Frustrated, she called Trevor.

"Hey, can you come over here and help me move my stuff inside?" Mya said, trying to keep her voice steady. "I don't know where Carter is, and I'm not about to let my stuff just sit outside in the yard."

There was a long pause before Trevor responded with a groggy, "Yeah, here I come."

"Alright, thanks," she said, trying to keep the irritation out of her voice.

She hung up and walked over to the window, pushing it open. The heat outside immediately rushed in, and she took a deep breath, trying to get some air circulation going. The sticky, humid air made her skin crawl, so she started to peel off her clothes. She couldn't deal with this heat anymore. After a few moments of struggle, she changed into something cooler, pulling on an old T-shirt and shorts.

Just as she tossed her old clothes on the sofa, her phone buzzed again. It was a text from Diana:

"Hey girl, First Lady's gonna be over soon to get fitted for her dress for the church ball. Thank you for this."

Mya wasn't ready for this. If there was one thing she could do, it was work. Work was the one thing that kept her from losing herself in everything else that seemed to be falling apart around her. Fixing her life wasn't something she was good at.

She picked up a water bottle from the fridge, cracked it open, and took a long, slow sip. Her eyes fell to the phone once more, but instead of replying to Diana, she set it face down on the table.

Trevor's footsteps echoed on the porch as he approached the door, his voice carrying through the frame. "This dude left your stuff outside."

Mya felt a sharp pang of frustration, her breath catching in her throat as she turned to face her brother. She had already seen the damage. She didn't need him to rub it in. "Don't start that mess, Trev, I can't take anything else," she said, trying to hold back the annoyance in her tone.

Trevor threw his hand up at her, a gesture that seemed to say, whatever, it's not my fault. Without waiting for a reply, he headed outside to start grabbing her bags and boxes.

Mya followed him onto the porch, wincing as she bent down to pick up her things. She had no desire to confront Carter just yet, and Trevor's comments weren't helping.

Trevor didn't miss a beat. "I know he's your husband, but you're my big sis and I'm always going to help you, but that's your husband. Common decency would be to take your wife's stuff inside." He glanced at her, raising an eyebrow as if daring her to argue.

Mya looked away, biting her lip. She wasn't ready to get into it, especially with Trevor. He always calling other people out but never handling his own mess.

Trevor was right, though. The least Carter could've done was bring in her things.

She helped Trevor move the bags into the house, one after another. After a while, they both paused outside for a moment to catch their breath. Trevor, ever the straight talker, didn't waste any time.

"Are you sure you want to stop your life to come back here? Like you got away why comeback?" Trevor asked, his voice softer now, almost concerned. He dropped a box on the ground, taking a step back and scanning the surroundings, as if seeing the house and neighborhood with fresh eyes. "I mean, look around nothing's changing."

Mya couldn't argue with him. The neighborhood had been like this for as long as she could remember, and the house... well, it was still the same place she'd left six years ago. She sighed, "I'm not here to move backwards, Trev. I missed y'all. I came back not just for Carter, but for all of us." she said, her voice steady despite the emotions stirring inside her. "I'm here to start something new...."

Her words felt like a promise to herself, even though she wasn't sure if she believed them entirely. Mya had to convince herself that this was part of the plan that she could make something new out of this old life.

Trevor eyed her with concern, but he didn't push it. He simply nodded, a quiet understanding in his gaze.

They continued moving the last of the boxes into the house. Finally, Trevor wiped his hands on his jeans, looking around the small living room. "Well, I don't know how we did it, but we did it. We fit all of that stuff in this little home. You sure you don't want to at least get another house out the hood?"

Mya laughed softly, the sound a little forced. "Then I wouldn't be able to be in your business now would I," she said, trying to keep it light.

Trevor looked at her like she better be lying.

Trevor sat down on the couch with a sigh, still looking uneasy. "So, sis..." He trailed off, leaning forward slightly. "You been in New York being this world class fashion designer, and Carter just been here chilling spending your funds with no job?"

Mya froze for a moment. She wasn't ready to answer that question. She had spent so many years pretending everything was fine, not wanting anyone to know how much she was carrying on her own. However, Trevor wasn't going to let it slide.

She couldn't avoid it anymore.

"Carter supports me and helps here he doesn't just spend all the money. What we have is deeper than just money" Mya said, the words feeling hollow as soon as they left her mouth. She hated that she had to say it out loud. She hated the shame that accompanied it.

Trevor shook his head slowly, his expression darkening. "So, basically, you're doing everything, and he's just living off you? He couldn't even bring your stuff in the house Mya." His voice was quiet but firm, like he was trying to break through the walls she had built around herself. "Now, Mya, grandma taught us better than this."

Mya's heart sank. She couldn't argue with him. Grandma had always been the strong one, so she is used to carrying the load for everybody.

"Grandma was single and alone, but when grandpa came back with nothing, she helped him." Mya said softly, as though the words might somehow make the situation better. "That's what I'm doing, helping my husband."

Before Trevor could respond, the door creaked open, and Carter walked in, his expression unreadable. He looked taken aback when he saw Trevor and Mya standing in the living room, surrounded by boxes and bags.

"Sorry," Carter said, his voice tight with surprise. "I'm not used to coming home to anybody." He barely made eye contact with Trevor, his arrogance practically oozing out of him.

Trevor stood up immediately, a grin spreading across his face as he extended his hand. "My main man, what's good?"

Carter froze for a moment, clearly unsure of how to react to his brother-in-law's overly friendly greeting. His gaze flicked between Mya and Trevor before landing on the ground. "What's up," he muttered, clearly uncomfortable.

Mya stayed quiet, her mind racing. She wasn't sure what to say or how to feel. Part of her wanted to defend Carter, so that Trevor wouldn't think things weren't as bad as they seemed. The other part of her—the part that had grown up watching strong, independent women knew this wasn't how things were supposed to be. Carter wasn't just living off her he was holding her back.

Trevor glanced around the cluttered living room, his eyes lingering on the stacked boxes and disheveled furniture. He realized he was invading space, so he let out a sigh. "I'm gonna head out," he muttered. He knew Mya and Carter needed some time.

As he was stepping out, the sound of a car pulling up caught his attention. The engine cut off, and the familiar voices of Diana and Tina could be heard from outside. Trevor peeked his head back through the door, his eyes flicking toward Mya.

"Step outside for a sec," he said, his tone softening slightly. He wasn't sure what Mya was dealing with, but he knew she needed support even if she didn't want to admit it.

Mya hesitated for a moment but then followed him to the door. When she stepped outside, the warmth of the late afternoon sun hit her, and she squinted against it. As soon as she caught sight of the car, she didn't know how to feel Carter was just getting home.

"Everything okay?" Mya asked, her voice laced with both concern and exhaustion.

"Girl, yes," Diana replied, leaning over the wheel, her hands still gripping the steering. "We just wanted to make sure you were good. You left kind of quick."

Mya gave a small shrug, glancing around the neighborhood. "Yes, I'm okay," she said, her gaze lingering on the house.

Tina leaned in her voice gentle but insistent. "We just wanted to make sure, because you were looking like you were ready to snap back there."

Mya's brow furrowed. "I just don't want to hear all the negative Carter comments right now."

"Girl, it is not like that, calm down," Tina interjected from the passenger seat, rolling her eyes. "You always getting riled up whenever anybody says something about him."

Mya let out a frustrated sigh. "Yeah, I do, he is my husband," she admitted, her attitude sharper now. "Do I ever say anything about Ray Ray?" She crossed her arms over her chest as her eyes narrowed.

Tina's head whipped toward her, her mouth dropping open in mock surprise. "I know you didn't just—" she started, but Mya wasn't finished.

"Yeah, I don't say anything about how he's got babies with everybody in the hood, do I?" Mya shot back; her voice laced with venom.

Tina's eyes widened in mock disbelief. "Oh, wow. We are going low I see," she retorted. "And I don't say anything about you giving Carter all your money while he lays up in your house and hasn't work a day in his life while you pay for everything," Tina snapped, the words spilling out before she could stop them.

Mya's jaw dropped as if she had been physically slapped. She sat frozen for a moment, processing what Tina had just said, before her lips twisted into a smirk. "Oh, so that's what we doing? I did not comeback for this right here" she said, her tone dripping with sarcasm.

Diana, who had been silently watching the back-andforth, finally spoke up, her voice a little frantic. "Y'all, please stop, we are better than this" she begged, her hands gripping the steering wheel tighter

Mya was done. She could feel the blood rush to her face, and her heart pounding with frustration. She gave a curt nod, walking away from the car with her head held high. "I don't have time for this" she muttered under her breath and headed back toward the house.

Diana stared at Mya's retreating form, then turned to Tina, her face full of concern. "You know, Tina, you couldn't just not say anything for once?"

Tina rolled her eyes, letting out a dramatic sigh. "It needed to be said." She shrugged, not even looking apologetic. "I'm just saying what everybody's thinking."

Diana threw her hands up in the air. "But why you gotta say it like that? You always go for the jugular, Tina. That ain't helping nobody."

Tina shot her a look, her eyes narrowing in a way that only she could do. "Mya can't keep acting like she's perfect all the time. She's the one who got herself into this situation with Carter, and now she's trying to act like nothing's wrong. I'm just calling it how I see it."

Diana sighed, her mind clearly conflicted. She knew Tina had a point. Carter had been a deadbeat for a while, and Mya had been the one carrying the weight of the relationship on her shoulders. But there was a right way to say things—and Tina's way wasn't it.

"I just wish you wouldn't be so harsh. I get it, but Mya's going through a lot right now. She doesn't need us making it harder for her." Diana shook her head, her voice softening.

Tina, unbothered, gave a casual shrug. "Well, I said what I had to say. She'll be fine. Besides she was bringing up stuff about me and you didn't say anything about that."

Mya stepped back inside the house, the door creaking as it shut behind her. The weight of the conversation with Diana and Tina still lingered in her spirit, and she was already feeling the pressure of trying to balance everything. She was ready for some peace, but when her eyes landed on Carter, sitting motionless on the couch, she felt her stomach twist in discomfort.

Carter didn't look up immediately, his thumb scrolling through something on his phone. The silence between them was thick, as if the years they'd spent together had finally become too heavy to carry in the same room.

"So.. how's everything been with you?" Mya finally asked.

Before he could answer, there was a knock at the door, sharp and unexpected.

Mya groaned. "Ugh, can't catch a break. Who could that be?" she muttered to herself. She walked to the door, her steps reluctant. When she swung it open, she found the social worker standing there with a wide smile plastered on her face.

"Hello, Mya! It's me again," the social worker greeted enthusiastically. "I have those documents for you to sign. Is it okay if I come in?"

Mya paused, her eyes darting back to Carter. Her stomach flipped, nerves beginning to tangle together. With a heavy sigh, she stepped back from the door and reluctantly let the social worker inside.

As the woman entered, Mya introduced her to Carter. "Carter, this is the social worker I've been working with," Mya said, her voice a little flat, trying to keep the mood neutral.

Carter glanced up briefly, his expression unreadable, before he stood up. "What's going on?" he asked, his tone tight, but Mya could feel the impatience behind it.

The social worker beamed, as if oblivious to the tension. "This is about the adoption," she replied brightly, though her voice carried a slight edge of uncertainty.

Mya's heart sank. She could feel Carter's gaze sharpen on her like a blade.

Carter's voice cut through the air, a mixture of confusion and frustration. "The adoption? Uhh, Mya, what is this?" His tone was louder now, almost accusatory.

Mya froze. The walls she had built around herself in the past few months felt like they were crumbling. She couldn't catch her breath. "I—I didn't want to tell you like this…" she stammered, but Carter's eyes were already narrowing with disbelief.

Before she could gather herself, the social worker looked between them, sensing the rising tension. "Is this a bad time?" she asked, looking hesitant.

Mya quickly stepped aside, signaling for her to come into the living room. "No, it's fine. Let's talk." Her voice was shaking, and she could feel her hands clenching at her sides.

She moved over to Carter, trying to stay calm, but her anxiety was eating at her. Carter's eyes never left her as he pulled Mya to the side, out of earshot of the social worker.

"What is going on, Mya?" Carter's voice was quiet, but the fury in his eyes was unmistakable. "You and all your surprises. You pop up back home with all your stuff, start a business, and now this?" His hand gestured toward the social worker in the other room. "What is this?"

Mya bit her lip, her mind racing to find the words. She wasn't prepared for any of this. Not for him to react like this, and certainly not to have all her decisions on full display. "Carter, I feel that since we can't have kids doesn't mean we can't have a family. This is the next best thing, and I know this can fix us" she said, her voice soft but filled with desperation. She could feel the weight of everything she had been trying to balance pressing down on her chest.

"This isn't how you do this, Mya. You can't just come back and expect everything to be the same and you can't bring a kid into all of this."

Carter's words were biting, and harsh. "Six years, Mya," he snapped, his voice rising now. "And now, in one day, you're trying to relive six years of our life together like it's just gonna magically fix everything? Like bringing a kid we know nothing about is going to make us a family I don't have to deal with this."

Mya could feel the ground beneath her shift. This was it—the moment she'd feared.

"I—I'm not asking you to fix everything in one day," Mya whispered, feeling like the smallest piece of herself was slipping away with each word. "I just need you to see it, see me. See how hard I'm trying to make everything work. I'm willing to do anything."

Before Carter could respond, the social worker stepped into the hallway, her voice cutting through the tense silence. "Do I need to come back another time?" she asked, looking between the two of them, her eyes darting nervously.

Mya glanced at Carter her throat tight. "No, no. We're ready," she said, almost too quickly, her eyes flicking nervously between the social worker and Carter. She gave him a pleading look, a silent request for him to let it go, if only for a moment.

Carter's jaw clenched, but he didn't say anything. He crossed his arms over his chest, a frown deepening on his face.

Mya could feel his resistance, could see the conflict in his posture, but she was too far gone in this moment to stop.

"Let's hear her out," Mya whispered to him, her voice barely above a breath. She wasn't sure if she was trying to convince him or herself, but she needed him to at least listen.

The social worker proceeded with her explanation of the adoption documents. Mya barely registered the words. Her mind was still spinning from the confrontation with Carter. When the social worker finally finished and handed Mya the papers to sign, Mya nodded absently. She felt as if she were in a fog, the weight of the past few days pressing down on her chest.

After the social worker left, Mya closed the door behind her, the silence in the house almost suffocating. Carter didn't move, his back turned to her, his arms still crossed tightly over his chest.

"Mya, I don't know what you've got going on, but this—this is not how you fix whatever this is," Carter said, his voice filled with anger and disappointment.

Mya's hands shook as she looked at him, her heart pounding. "Now you finally admit there's something wrong with us?" she asked, the bitterness creeping into her words.

Carter's face reddened, and his eyes narrowed as he stepped closer to her. "Six years, Mya. Six years of this. And now, in one day, you're trying to relive it all. I don't see how you think that is possible and then you want to create a family?"

The pain of his words hit her harder than she expected. He had been distant for so long, but this… this felt like the final nail in the coffin. She swallowed hard, but her voice was still quiet. "Wait, Carter, please. We have so much to look forward to. Yes, it's been six years, but it doesn't have to end" she said, her words spilling out in a desperate plea. "This is important. We must make this work."

Carter's face twisted in frustration. "That's your problem, Mya, I never asked for that. I never asked for any of this" he snapped, before turning away.

With those final words, Carter stormed out of the house, leaving Mya standing alone in the silence. The echo of his steps on the floor felt deafening. She stood there for a moment, her chest rising and falling rapidly, trying to catch her breath.

There was nothing left to say.

Chapter 5
REDEMPTION

Mya stood frozen for a moment, staring at the door that Carter had just slammed behind him. Her mind was a storm of thoughts, racing faster than she could catch them. Why did he have to leave like that? What did he mean, "I don't have to deal with this?" The weight of his words pressed against her chest, but the sting wasn't new. It felt like an old wound opening, one she hadn't realized was still there, still bleeding.

She had barely processed his exit when there was another knock at the door. Her heart leapt with a small glimmer of hope, but when she opened it and saw Diana standing on the other side, that hope deflated like a punctured balloon.

"Oh, it's just you," Mya muttered, trying to hide her disappointment, though it was impossible to mask the exhaustion in her voice.

Diana looked at her with raised eyebrows. "Dang, hello to you." But the sharp edge in her voice softened as she stepped into the room. "You good girl?" she asked, the concern in her eyes genuine, even if her tone was teasing.

Mya didn't answer right away. Instead, she let out a long, frustrated sigh and flopped onto the couch. "What do you think?" she grumbled, staring up at the ceiling like it held all the answers she was too afraid to ask for.

Diana didn't push her, but just as she opened her mouth to say something comforting, another knock came at the door.

"That must be First Lady," Diana said, rising to her feet.

Mya groaned, the weight of everything pressing down even harder now. She wasn't sure if she was ready for any more deep conversations today, but when the door swung open and First Lady walked in, her loud, cheerful voice filled the space.

"My God, My God! It's hotter than Satan's pit, I know I'm living right for the rest of my life! How are y'all doing?" she declared, her eyes twinkling as she stepped in like she was on a mission from Heaven.

Mya felt the smallest flicker of irritation. She didn't feel like pretending to be okay. She didn't even feel like engaging with First Lady's infectious optimism. "Let me get my stuff," she mumbled, already walking toward the back of the house.

Diana, sensing the tension, quickly stepped in. "I'm sorry. She's still getting settled," she said to First Lady, her voice apologetic but firm.

First Lady looked at her understandingly and nodded. "I understand, honey. She turned back to Mya as she re-entered the room and smiled warmly. "I know your grandma is smiling from heaven—how proud she must be of you."

Mya's face twitched, her attitude sharp. "Are you so sure about that?" she shot back, bitterness creeping into her voice.

First Lady's smile faltered for a second, then she looked at Diana for a moment before returning her gaze to Mya. "I sure do. Don't you think so?" she asked gently. "This is what she prayed for, and I know God is proud."

Mya crossed her arms over her chest, her frustration bubbling up. "Please, don't talk about that in here. I don't believe in that." Her voice was heavy with doubt.

Diana glanced at First Lady, her eyebrows furrowing with concern. “Well, who do you believe in then?” she asked softly, her eyes filled with a mix of curiosity and worry.

Mya sighed and turned looking her in the eyes smiling. “Not who, it’s what,” she muttered. “I believe in love.” Her voice was tinged with hopelessness. She had given so much to love, and yet here she was broken, confused, and unsure of what was next.

First Lady laughed but didn’t flinch at Mya’s words. Her voice softened as she responded, “Baby, God is love. You’ve got to know that, and when you surrender yourself to Him you will experience it. He’s the one who shows up when nobody else will.”

Mya threw her hands up, frustration pouring out of her like a broken dam. "Well, where is He, then? Where is He? My whole life is falling apart. My marriage is crumbling. I have nowhere to go, and I don’t know what to do!" She couldn’t hold it in anymore. The tears were right there, threatening to spill over, but her pride held them back, just barely.

First Lady made a lighthearted joke, trying to diffuse the tension. “Well, did you call love?” she said, her tone teasing but kind.

Mya blinked, her mouth tightening in disbelief. First Lady couldn’t have just said that. When she saw the humor in the older woman’s eyes, she became enraged and crossed her arms.

“I’m kidding, honey,” First Lady said with a wink. “All I’m saying is, love didn’t get up and die on a cross for you. God did that. He’s the one who can help you when you feel like you’ve hit rock bottom.”

Diana nodded in agreement, her eyes full of conviction.

"Amen, Mya. You need to wake up, sis, and take your home back. You need to allow God to take control, but you also need to give your life over to God. Let Him do what He does best."

Mya felt a strange mixture of relief and confusion. "But… how?" she whispered.

First Lady's voice softened with compassion. "You need to submit, Mya. Submit to God and surrender your heart. Then, you fight for your marriage. You fight for your home. You know what God has joined together, no man can tear apart. You hear me?"

Mya felt hope rise. She nodded slowly. "Yes, ma'am."

"Don't let this industry change you, or what you seen your grandma go through" First Lady continued, her voice gentle but firm. "Don't think it's you, baby, It's God's grace. It's God who brought you back home to work on your marriage. If this was you, you would have been back. This right here is all God. You give your life over to God, and He will take care of everything. You pray over your home, and you rejoin with your husband. God is where your peace will come from."

Diana reached over, rubbing Mya's shoulder gently. "You can do this, Mya. You don't have to do it alone."

Mya's heart felt lighter, and for the first time in a long time, she allowed herself to cry—not in despair, but in surrender. She let the tears fall freely, tears that she hadn't even realized she had been holding back. She was tired. Tired of trying to control everything, tired of carrying the weight of the world on her shoulders. For once, it felt okay to just let go.

Diana gently pulled her into a hug, her voice soft as she began to pray for her, for her marriage, and for her strength to move forward with faith.

Mya's heart softened, and as Diana prayed, she felt a sense of peace wash over her that she hadn't felt in years. It wasn't an immediate fix, but it was a start. It was a first step.

As the prayer ended, Mya wiped her eyes and looked over at First Lady, who was now standing in front of the mirror, admiring herself.

"Well, I'm a heavy-set plus-size fine First Lady, so don't judge the curves," she said with a wink, laughing at herself. "That's how Pastor likes it."

Mya and Diana burst out laughing. For the first time all day, the tension in the room lifted.

Chapter 6
THE BEGINNING

Mya stood in front of her mirror, carefully applying her makeup. Despite the chaos swirling in her mind, she forced herself to smile. Tonight was important. It was supposed to be a celebration her new business, her fresh start, the possibility of something new and exciting. The emptiness in her heart made it hard to enjoy the moment. Still, she pressed on, determined to look her best, even if it was just for herself.

Her phone buzzed on the counter, and when she glanced at it, a small smile tugged at her lips. It was a message from Chase, letting her know that her dog was doing fine.

At least something's right in my life, Mya thought as she put the phone down tying the final knot in her dress and smoothing it out. She took a deep breath, wiped away the last of her worries, and headed to the store.

When she arrived, she was immediately struck by how beautiful the space looked. London had done an incredible job.

"London, oh my Lord, you have it beautiful in here!" Mya exclaimed, a genuine smile stretching across her face. The place was transformed—warm, inviting, and elegant. It was everything Mya had dreamed of, and more.

Trevor burst through the back door, acting like he was part of the magic. "It wasn't just her; it was me too."

London rolled her eyes but kept it lighthearted. "All he did was move some chairs, That's it."

Trevor shot her a mock glare. "Shut up, that's something."

The atmosphere lightened with laughter, but it was short-lived as Tina swaggered in, her heels clicking against the floor. "Heyyyy, y'all! Where everybody at?" she called out, her energy filling the room.

Mya couldn't help but laugh. "Girl, you're early! But you look gorgeous."

Tina grinned, strutting over to Mya. "Of course I do," she replied, as if it were a fact.

Trevor shook his head with a smirk. "You better be careful with all that confidence. You'll break the floor."

Before Tina could respond, Diana walked in, her calm presence making the room feel more grounded. She looked around and raised an eyebrow at Tina. "Girl, you could've worn anything, but that?" Diana teased, her hand on her hip.

Tina gave Diana a pointed look. "Do you have to look holy everywhere you go?"

Diana made a face, then responded, "You need to start looking holy."

The two exchanged playful jabs, but Diana was quick to walk up and hug Mya. "It looks wonderful in here," she said, admiring the space.

The door swung open, and the first customer walked in a well-dressed woman with a confidence about her.

"Is this our first customer?" London asked, her eyes wide with excitement.

London quickly approached her. "Hello, welcome to our grand opening. Please feel free to look around, and if you need any assistance, I'm here."

The woman, introducing herself as Tracy, glanced around before looking directly at London. "Is Mya here?" she asked, a strange tone in her voice.

London gave a polite smile. "Yes, she's over there, but she's busy now. Would you like me to let her know you're here?"

Tracy raised an eyebrow and made a face. "No, No I just wanted to know if she was here for her grand opening I heard a lot about her." she replied before walking out.

London shook her head, watching her go. "Guess she didn't want anything," she muttered under her breath.

The door opened again, and Carter walked in. Mya's heart skipped.

"Oh, hey, Mya," stopping in his tracks when he spotted her, his tone somewhat distant.

Mya stood still for a moment, eyeing him. "Well, hey to you Carter, uhm .... where are your clothes, Carter?"

He glanced down at his attire—clearly not the sharp, put-together look that the event required. "I didn't have time to change, sorry," he said dismissively.

Mya raised an eyebrow, irritated. "I think I have something in the back," she said coldly.

As they walked toward the back of the store, the rest of the guests began to trickle in—First Lady and Pastor, followed by a lively crowd of churchgoers and community members.

In the back Mya turned toward Carter. "Here you go, I can't believe you came here not dress, seriously. What is up with you" she whispered.

Before he could answer, he stormed out of the back room. Mya screamed his name, her voice filled with desperation.

"Carter!"

She ran to the front of the store, but First Lady, sensing the tension, pulled her aside. "Don't worry, sweetheart. Everything will turn around. Just wait. This is only the beginning."

Mya stood frozen, unsure of what was happening. Then suddenly, Tracy walked back in.

London quickly greeted her with a forced smile. "Welcome back…again" she said with a slightly sarcastic edge.

Tina turned to Mya, raising an eyebrow. "You need to teach her how to talk to people," she whispered.

Before Mya could respond, Carter stormed back in, his face twisted in frustration. He looked directly at Tracy. "Baby, I thought I told you to wait in the car."

Tina, standing nearby, couldn't hold back. "Baby?" she repeated, her voice dripping with disbelief. "Your wife right here, and I haven't heard you call her baby since she been back!"

Mya was shaking now, her heart pounding in her chest. "Carter, what is going on?" she asked, her voice cracking with fear.

Tracy stepped forward, and with a cold, unwavering gaze, she looked directly at Mya. "Carter, tell her." Mya's stomach dropped.

Carter glanced at Tracy, then back at Mya, his eyes filled with an odd mix of guilt and defiance. "I'm sorry you have to find out this way, Mya," he said, his voice emotionless.

Mya was too stunned to speak. The world around her seemed to blur as the words hit her like a freight train.

Tina's voice cut through the shock. "What is this boy got going on?" she demanded, stepping toward him.

Carter stood strong and bold and looked Tina in the eye. "You stay out of it. We don't have time for your loudmouth right now."

Mya's hands trembled as she tried to process what was happening. Carter turned to her, his expression unreadable. "Mya, this is just the way it is now. You've been doing your thing, so it's time for me to do mine. I'm taking my half, and you can keep yours."

Tina's eyes widened, her disbelief palpable. "Half!? What half!? You didn't put in on any of this!" she shouted, her voice rising in anger.

Carter, dismissing her, looked back at Mya. "Remember what you said? This is both of ours."

Tracy stepped forward again, her voice cold. "I see some changes I want to make."

Mya's chest tightened as she tried to find her words. "Changes? This is too much. So, this is what you've been doing, cheating on me? With everything I've done for you and then you bring her in my store!

Carter looked over at Mya, his eyes filled with rage—but not just anger. It was the kind of fury that had been simmering, unspoken, buried beneath silence and restraint. This wasn't about what was happening now. It was about everything he hadn't said.

"When will you stop trying to control me," he said sharply, "and be my wife?"

His voice cracked slightly, but his face remained stone cold.

"Truth be told… I lost my wife a long time ago. I stopped being your husband and started being your baggage. And that—" he paused, jabbing his finger toward the ground for emphasis, "that right there is not what I'm going to be."

He gestured toward the woman standing off to the side. "Now this woman—we might be in the wrong. I can admit that, but she does the things you never even thought about doing."

"Why?" he asked, voice rising. "Because your dreams mattered more than the love we could share."

His voice broke now, and the pain spilled out with it. "I never wanted this… I never wanted *any* of this."

Mya stepped forward, her voice firm but shaking. "But all of this—everything right here—it took care of you!"

Carter stared at her, breathing hard. Then he nodded slowly. "You may be right. Actually, you are right, but shouldn't it?"

He stepped closer, eyes narrowing.

"I'm trapped in your web. So, it might as well feed me."

A tear slipped down Mya's cheek.

Carter turned to leave but paused at the door. Without turning around, Mya yelled, "She'll never put up with the crap I put up with. Trust me she'll be gone faster than I can snap my fingers."

He threw his hand up, dismissing the moment, without another word.

Carter grabbed Tracy by the arm and began to walk out, his footsteps heavy and deliberate. Mya fell to her knees, the weight of his words crashing over her like a tidal wave.

Her breath hitched as tears spilled from her eyes. She couldn't breathe. She couldn't think.

"Carter…" she whispered, as the reality of everything they'd built together unraveled in front of her eyes.

The door creaked open, and Chase stepped into the shop, his usual confident stride now slowed as he took in the scene before him. His eyes scanned the room, and it didn't take long for him to realize that a storm had just swept through there.

Mya stood up near the counter, her hands shaking slightly as she tried to pull herself together. The damage was done. Her heart was broken, shattered into pieces by the very man she'd built her world around.

First Lady, who had been standing by Mya's side, gently placed a hand on her shoulder. "Baby, you dare blame yourself," she said, her voice soft but strong, "You must be strong now. This is the time to lean on God, and on the people who love you."

Mya's eyes welled up, her voice cracking as she spoke.

"I don't know where I went wrong, First Lady. I always chose him first. I always took care of us, and this is what he does? He just... throws it all away." Her words were heavy, laden with hurt and disbelief.

First Lady squeezed her shoulder, offering comfort in silence for a moment. She could see the depth of Mya's pain. This wasn't just about a relationship it was about the years Mya had invested in a man who now seemed to have no regard for her.

London, who had been quietly observing the scene, made her way toward Chase. He had placed the flowers he'd been holding on the counter when he first walked in. His posture was stiff, his gaze distant.

"What's wrong?" Chase asked gently, his voice low, worried.

London looked over at Mya and back at Chase and sighed. "Mya's husband... he just told her he has a whole new woman" London said in disbelief.

Chase glanced back at Mya, who was barely holding it together, her tears streaming down her face.

London didn't know what to think. This was the whole reason Mya and her even came down south, so that Mya can work on her marriage with her husband.

Mya was still trying to process it all, still reeling from the blow. It wasn't just Carter's words that hurt. It was the life they'd built together the plans they'd made. All of it now reduced to ashes.

Then, as if on cue Carter walked back in, and Mya's heart skipped a beat. Why was he back? Had he come to explain? To apologize? His cold demeanor said otherwise.

She looked at him, her voice barely a whisper as she tried to steady herself. "Can we talk, Carter?"

He didn't answer her, he barely even looked at her. Just grabbed his keys and made his way across the room. Mya's pulse quickened, her emotions warring inside her hurt, anger, desperation.

Carter looked back at Mya, his gaze cold, emotionless, before he turned and walked out the door without saying a word. The door closed behind him with a finality that felt deafening. Mya stood there, frozen, her body trembling from the shock of it all.

"I just don't understand. I gave him everything… all of me, and this is what he does. How could he do this to me?" Her voice cracked, and she collapsed into the chair, her body wracked with sobs.

First Lady's voice broke through the silence, her words gentle yet firm. "Mya, you've done nothing wrong. You can't blame yourself for this. People change. Sometimes, they make choices that hurt the ones they love. That doesn't mean you have to carry this burden alone."

Mya wiped her tears, slowly nodding as she tried to steady her breath. "I know. I know. It just doesn't feel real."

Mya managed a faint smile. It wasn't much, but it was something. She looked up at Chase, who stood quietly nearby, his hands still in his pockets.

She took a deep breath and glanced toward the door. Carter was gone, but maybe that wasn't such a bad thing. It hurt. The pain was unbearable, but maybe it was time to let go.

She had built her world around him, thinking they'd be different, that she'd be different—not like her grandma, not like the other women in her family who had sacrificed so much for men who never returned the favor. Mya had vowed she'd never become a doormat in a relationship, yet here she was, paying for a man who couldn't even lift a finger to stand beside her.

The door had barely closed behind Carter when her friends and family rushed in to offer support. Even the people who loved her couldn't fill the emptiness left behind by his betrayal.

Tina's voice broke through Mya's spiraling thoughts as she turned her head to Chase, who had quietly entered the room earlier. Tina raised an eyebrow and looked him up and down, a mischievous grin forming on her face.

"Who is this man?" Tina asked, her tone dripping with curiosity.

Chase glanced around the room, still trying to process everything that had happened. He gave a soft smile, his presence calm and steady. "I'm Mya's friend, Chase. We worked together in New York," he said, a little sheepish.

Tina's eyes narrowed, sizing him up as if she were trying to gauge what kind of man he was. After a long pause, she clicked her tongue, "Well, I guess Mya's been doing her thing as well. Mhm, mhm."

Chase laughed softly, trying to brush off the attention. "Oh, no. It's nothing like that. We both work in the fashion industry, just on different sides of it. Close work friends," he clarified quickly.

Tina's eyes twinkled mischievously. "Oh, you gay?"

Chase blinked, slightly taken aback, but then chuckled. "Not every man in the fashion industry is gay" he said, smiling broadly.

Tina tilted her head and grinned. "Well, good, cause you fine." She batted her lashes at him, but Chase merely shook his head and smiled, clearly not interested in entertaining Tina's flirtations.

Diana, ever the voice of reason, nudged Tina and whispered, "What about Ray Ray?"

Tina scoffed, rolling her eyes. "What about him? Ray Ray out here doing God knows what."

London, who had been standing near the counter, couldn't resist a little jibe. "Didn't you just shoot him in the leg the other day for cheating?"

Tina turned toward her sharply, her expression turning icy. "For someone not from here, you sure do know my business."

London stepped back; hands raised defensively. "I—I was just asking," she said, looking nervous as Tina's gaze became more intense.

Before anything else could happen, Mya suddenly started ruffling through her things. Her hands trembled, and her heart raced. The moment with Carter was hitting her harder than she realized.

First Lady, ever the calm presence, tried to offer Mya some comfort. "Baby, take a breath," she said gently.

Mya wasn't having it. "I can't, I can't take the side conversations and just all of this. Thank you all for coming." she snapped, rushing out of the room before anyone could stop her.

Trevor, who had been quietly stewing in the corner, suddenly stormed toward the door. His fury was palpable. "I'm about to go handle him. I don't know what he's thinking, doing my sister like that," he spat, his voice sharp with anger.

Pastor, sensing trouble, hurried after him. "Trevor, wait! Don't do something you'll regret," he called out, his voice full of concern.

As Trevor and Pastor left, First Lady began praying, her voice rising as she called out to God, her words filled with urgency. "Lord, we need you. We need you to come down and shift this atmosphere! Bring peace where there is chaos. Heal the broken hearts in this room, Lord, in Jesus' name!"

Diana, beside First Lady, joined in, her voice soft at first but growing with authority. "Lord, we lift Mya up to you. You are the healer of broken hearts. Let her find strength in your love and grace. Help her to see the path you have set before her, to find peace in the midst of her storm."

The two women stood in agreement, interceding for Mya, for her marriage, for the brokenness she was feeling.

Tina, on the other hand, stood in the background, eyeing Chase with interest. She wasn't interested in the situation with Mya—at least, not completely. She had a different agenda, as always. Tina didn't bother hiding the way her eyes roamed over Chase's form as he and London spoke, their conversation light and easy.

"So, Miss Thang, Miss London, you and Chase together or what?" Tina called out, her voice dripping with her usual mischief.

London and Chase looked at each other, and both broke into laughter, the tension in the room briefly lifting.

"No, we aren't together," London said, her voice amused but tinged with a hint of confusion. "And what's it to you?"

Diana, who had been busy cleaning up the mess from earlier and praying, shot Tina a look that spoke volumes. "Tina," she said, her voice low but firm. "Don't make me get my oil."

Tina raised her hands in mock surrender, a big smile playing on her lips. "What? I was just asking, you need to be asking I haven't seen you with a man in 30 years you must plan on marrying Jesus" she said innocently, though it was clear from the twinkle in her eye that she was enjoying the attention.

Chase, not missing a beat, leaned in slightly, his deep voice smooth. "I can help wherever you need me," he said with a smile, his tone teasing but genuine.

Tina's eyes lit up at the comment, and she wasted no time. "Oh, you sure can," she said, her flirtation unmistakable.

First Lady, who had been praying and speaking in tongues just moments ago, couldn't help but roll her eyes at Tina's antics. She turned her gaze toward Tina, her tone firm and stern. "Tina don't make me start praying about you and cast that lust demon out," she warned, her voice filled with authority.

Tina froze for a moment, her playful expression faltering. First Lady's words carried weight, and Tina knew better than to test her. She cleared her throat and glanced over at Chase, finally easing up. "Alright, alright. I'm just playing."

Chase chuckled under his breath, but he didn't seem fazed by Tina's flirting.

Chapter 7
THE WEIGHT

Approaching home, Mya sat in her car, her heart aching with a pain she couldn't seem to escape. The weight of everything that had happened over the last few days pressed down on her, suffocating her. She could still see Carter's face, still hear his voice as he walked away with another woman, leaving her in a cloud of confusion and heartbreak.

She sat there for what felt like hours, the tears coming in waves, but it was only when the last of them dried up that she found the strength to leave the car. The house felt cold, almost like a stranger's home, empty and vast.

Stepping inside, Mya was met with darkness. Not just from the absence of light, but from the coldness that seemed to permeate every corner of the space. She stood there for a moment, trying to gather herself, but it felt like her world was spinning. The echo of her own footsteps seemed to mock her as she walked further in, every room a reminder of the life that was slipping away.

Then, the scream came. It was raw, desperate, a howl from the deepest part of her soul. It was the kind of scream that only came when there was nothing left to give. No more hope. No more fight.

She collapsed onto the floor, curling up into a ball as if to hide from the world and the pain that had overtaken her. For days she laid there consumed by the void of her own grief. The house felt as though it was swallowing her whole, the silence louder than any words could have been. People came to check on her Diana, Tina, even First Lady, but Carter never did. That hurt more than she cared to admit.

A couple days passed, and the world outside continued as if nothing had changed. For Mya everything had shifted, and the weight of it all seemed unbearable.

Finally, on the third day, she dragged herself out of bed, feeling like a ghost in her own life. She reached for her phone, the weight of the missed calls flashing in front of her. Chase. There were so many from him, but none from Carter. The realization stung again.

Mya hesitated for a moment, her finger hovering over the screen before she called Chase back.

"Hey," she said when he picked up. Her voice was weak, as though it had been trapped in her throat for days.

“Mya,” Chase greeted warmly, but she could hear the concern in his voice. “I’ve been trying to reach you. Do you need anything?”

Mya took a deep breath, trying to steady herself. “I’m sorry,” she said, her voice breaking just a little. “I hate you had to experience all of that. I didn’t even get to spend any time with you when you were here.”

Chase didn’t hesitate. “It’s okay,” he reassured her. “I understand. You’ve got a lot going on, and I’m still here.”

Mya wiped a tear away, a small smile forming on her face despite the heaviness in her chest. “Thank you, Chase. You still here? How about we meet up? There’s this little spot that has the best breakfast ever.”

He laughed lightly, the sound bringing a small measure of comfort. “Let’s do it,” he said. “Text me the location.”

Mya stepped out of the shower, the hot water having done little to soothe the ache deep within her bones. She stood in front of the bathroom mirror, taking a long look at herself. The face staring back at her looked familiar, but the eyes were different—darker, more tired. The weight of the last few days had taken its toll, but she refused to let it break her.

She reached for her body lotion and began to moisturize her skin, the routine comforting in its simplicity. As she moved, she whispered a quiet prayer.

"God, I know I'm probably the last person you want to hear from, but I need You. I need Your strength, your guidance. I can't do this on my own. I surrender my life and all of this to You. I place it in Your hands."

The words felt like a weight lifted from her chest, though the pain in her heart remained. Mya took a deep breath and grabbed her phone and keys. She walked outside, stepping into the sunlight. The neighborhood was alive kids running through the streets, men laughing and joking around, the sound of life resuming as if nothing had changed. It was a stark contrast to the heaviness she felt inside.

As Mya walked to her car she was stopped by a familiar voice.

"Mya Wright? Is that you?"

She turned to see an old childhood friend standing across the street, grinning like they'd never been apart.

"Damon Fears?!" Mya gasped, unable to hide the surprise in her voice. She hadn't seen Damon in years, not since high school.

Damon chuckled and crossed the street, extending his arms for a hug. "It's really you! Man, it's been forever. How've you been?"

Mya smiled as he wrapped her in a warm embrace. "It's good to see you, Damon." She pulled away to take a better look at him. He'd grown into a confident, successful man. His t-shirt sported the logo of his own delivery company something she hadn't expected but found inspiring.

"What are you doing back here? I thought you were living it up in New York," Damon asked, curious.

Mya looked down, feeling a pang in her chest as she thought about how things had spiraled. "I came back to start something new... to figure things out," she said softly. "What about you? I see you're doing big things."

Damon stepped back, puffing out his chest with pride. "Yep, yep. Ya boy's out here making some moves with my own delivery company. Big moves, you know?"

Mya laughed, impressed. "Wow, D. That's amazing. You're killing it. I never thought you would do delivery work."

Damon grinned wide, clearly pleased with himself. "It's been a journey, but I'm happy with where I'm at. It's been good for me." He nodded in her direction, his smile softening. "It's good to see you again, Mya. I got to get back to these loads. I'm glad to see you back in the neighborhood."

Mya watched him head back to his truck, a bit of awe in her heart. She had always admired Damon's drive, and it was clear he was still on top of his game. She waved as he drove off, then turned and headed for her car, making her way to the diner.

The Sunny Soul food diner was a quaint little place that seemed to have been frozen in time. The smell of bacon, pancakes, and strong coffee filled the air, and the clinking of silverware on plates mixed with the chatter of the few patrons scattered around. It was the kind of place that made you feel like grandma was in the kitchen, cooking up love in every bite.

Mya spotted Chase already sitting at a booth near the window, his casual demeanor providing a sense of calm that she appreciated. She walked over and greeted him with a side hug, grateful for the sense of normalcy he brought.

"Hey there," Chase said warmly. "How're you feeling today?"

Mya smiled faintly, trying to mask the lingering pain. "Better, I guess. Still taking it day by day."

The waitress couldn't have been more than twenty. She approached their table, chewing gum loudly and sporting a pencil behind her ear with a bright pink lipstick that screamed "sassy." Looking Mya up and down before asking, "What can I get y'all to drink, boo?"

"I'll have a water and a coffee—black, please. I like to add my own cream and sugar," she said.

Chase glanced at Mya and then said, "Same for me."

The waitress walked off with a snap of her gum, and Mya turned to Chase. "I have to get it out, I am sorry about what happened yesterday," she said, the weight of it all in her voice. "I didn't mean for it to turn into... well, whatever that was. I wanted it to be something of joy."

Chase sighed, shaking his head. "Trust me I know that's not what you wanted. It's fine. Well, not fine, but you'll get through it. One thing I know about you is that you always end up on top."

She offered a small smile. "I don't feel strong right now," she admitted. "But I'm trying."

Chase smiled back. "That's all anyone can do. Just try."

Mya grabbed a menu, trying to distract herself. "This menu is a long way from New York," she said with a playful smirk.

Chase laughed. "Yeah, the South is a different world, quiet and peaceful."

Mya nodded. "Yeah, it's nice, It's home."

As they chatted, Chase's phone buzzed, and he excused himself to take the call. Mya used the time to check her phone. No messages from Carter. Nothing at all.

When Chase returned, they joked around about nothing, trying to keep the mood light. Mya could feel the weight of his unspoken words. She knew he cared, but she couldn't allow herself to feel more for him right now. Not when her heart was still fractured from everything with Carter.

When breakfast was over, they both stood up and exchanged goodbyes. "I'll see you around, Mya. Take care of yourself, okay?" Chase said, his voice kind but tinged with something deeper.

Mya nodded, grateful. "I will. Thanks for coming out to see me I know it wasn't the best, but thank you for always supporting."

She headed to the boutique, still trying to hold herself together. As she walked in, she noticed there were customers inside, the place buzzing with life. Word had gotten around about what had happened at the grand opening, but the business was still going on.

London greeted her with a warm smile before heading off to assist a customer. Mya watched, still in awe of how London had turned everything around. Just a few days ago, this place had felt like the last thing she wanted to hold onto, but now—now it felt like a lifeline.

She walked into her office and sat down, trying to center herself. That's when London came in with exciting news. "Mya, a publicist is here!" she said, practically glowing. "They want to do some photo ops of the boutique, show the big changes. This is big!"

Mya blinked in surprise. "A publicist?" She wasn't sure what to make of it, but as she stood up and followed London out front, she saw the small surprise that Chase had left for her: a handwritten note on the desk. It read:

"Bad times come, but they set the scene for good things to flow. You got this! Time to blow this business up"

A tear slipped down Mya's cheek as she read the words. She smiled, feeling a flicker of hope ignite inside her. Chase had believed in her when she couldn't even believe in herself.

Chapter 8
CARTER

Carter was knocked out, deep in sleep, when Tracy walked into the small room, he now called home. She nudged him. "Wake up baby, it's 1 p.m."

He groaned, turning over. "Alright, alright," he mumbled, dragging himself up. He'd been up all night playing the game, lost in a virtual world where responsibilities didn't exist.

Tracy headed to the kitchen, and a few moments later, Carter followed. He leaned against the counter, stretching. "When you plan on cleaning this place?"

Tracy didn't miss a beat. "When you plan on going to work?"

Carter smirked, walking up behind her and kissing her cheek before sauntering over to the table. Tracy shook her head but smiled, handing him a glass of orange juice.

"So," she said, leaning back against the counter, arms crossed. "What's the next step for you and ole girl?"

Carter scoffed, taking a sip. "I ain't even thinking about that—or her. She wasn't worried about me so why should I worry about her. I'm just going to live in the moment."

Tracy's smile faded. "You need to worry about that. We need some money. We can't both live off my child support checks and food stamps."

Carter glanced at his phone, then back at her. "I got this. Don't worry."

He dialed Jamal's number. After a few rings, his friend picked up, background noise signaling he was at work.

"Aye, bruh."

Jamal sighed. "Man, I heard about what you did to Mya. You know Nancy ain't gon' want me talking to you."

"Man, hush. I need a favor."

"What's up?"

"I need you to help me move my stuff."

Jamal exhaled hard. "Oh no, no, no. I can't do that. You know me and Mya cool. I can't get in the middle of that, bruh. I'm sorry."

Carter clenched his jaw. "I thought you were my dog."

"I am. I just can't get in the middle."

"Then why you are showing her more loyalty than me?"

Jamal sighed. "Because, fool, you had it good, and you messed that up. I wish Nancy would let me be a stay-at-home husband. I would've become a full-time mannequin for her."

"Bye, bruh. I ain't trying to hear that." Carter ended the call, shaking his head.

Tracy looked up from her phone. "Who was that?"

"Just my homie."

She walked over, draping her arms around his shoulders. "Am I ever gonna meet this homie?"

Carter looked away, forcing a smile. "Yeah, most def, bae."

Tracy grinned. "I'm so glad you chose me and stuck up for our family."

Carter squeezed her hands. "I told you, I got us. Mya wasn't looking at me like her husband. I was her accessory. It's not like that over here."

She beamed, the kind of flash that could make a man forget everything else. Tracy was vibrant, where Mya had been subtle. Tracy made him feel needed, and wanted.

His phone buzzed. Jamal had sent a text.

I can't believe you left your beautiful wife for ugly, big-booty Tracy, man.

Carter flipped his phone over before Tracy could see.

She pulled away. "What are you getting into today?"

"Probably go over to the house, get my stuff, then chill here."

Tracy leaned against the counter. "So when you think I'm gonna get the boutique, because I have things I want to change? I'm so ready to get in there!"

Carter sighed, walking toward the couch. "Real soon, babe. Ima talk to her about that real soon."

People had a lot to say about Tracy, but one thing was for sure she was available, and that's what Carter needed. Mya was always off chasing her dreams, leaving him alone. He begged her not to go, but she did what she wanted, like always. Tracy might not be rich, but at least she was there.

Tracy grabbed her purse. "I'm about to run to the store."

They exchanged a quick kiss before she left. The place was much smaller than where he was before, but at least he wasn't alone. They'd get something better soon.

Carter threw on his running shoes and headed to the park for his daily run. He wasn't proud of how things had gone down. He wasn't proud of leaving Mya, or what he did at her shop. He actually wanted to tell her everything after he had things sorted. He loved Mya—he just fell out of love with her.

His phone buzzed again. His mama. He ignored it. He didn't know how to explain any of this to her. This wasn't how she raised him. Eight years of marriage and six of them with Mya off in New York. They tried to make it work, but he begged her not to leave. She did anyway.

As he reached town, he stopped by the corner store and ran into Ray Ray. They knew each other through mya and tina friendship.

Ray Ray smirked. "Man, I heard you blew the spot up the other day."

Carter grabbed a water bottle. "Man, it wasn't even supposed to go down like that."

Ray Ray chuckled. "It went down the way it had to. They love to ambush us."

Carter exhaled. "Yeah, you right man. I bet all of them talking about me."

Ray Ray rang him up. "Oh, you know they are. That's all they know to do. I'm just glad I ain't the one they are talking about right now."

Carter nodded. "Man, I'm out of that group now. Got a new woman. New chance at life."

Ray Ray raised an eyebrow. "So, you are staying with Tracy?"

"Yeah, man. Might as well."

Ray Ray shrugged. "I guess, bro. watch your back with her. Trust me I know how she is."

Carter nodded at ray ray took his water. He had to figure out when to grab his stuff from the house without running into Mya or her friends. He just wanted a clean break.

On the way home, he stopped by Jamal's job. Jamal spotted him and walked over. "My cheatin' brotha."

Carter rolled his eyes. "Man, shut up."

Jamal shook his head. "I can't believe you did it, man."

Carter shrugged. "It's really not that bad."

Jamal frowned. "Bruh, people saying they ain't seen Mya in days. The girl just got here and got the wind knocked out of her."

Carter looked away, his stomach twisting.

Jamal sighed. "She was a good woman. I could never do that to Nancy."

Carter smirked. "Because she'd kill you."

Jamal laughed. "That's what I love about her—she doesn't play about her man."

Carter shook his head. "See, if me and Mya had that, we'd be alright."

Jamal got serious. "What you talking about yall did have that bro, that girl moved her life here. Man, you think you made the right decision?"

Carter sat down on the bench. "She moved her life here our life was never supposed to be separate. Money ain't everything. I really think I did what's best for me. I'm not saying a woman can't have dreams."

Jamal interrupts. "Yeah, somebody gotta work and pay bills."

Carter made a face. "Man, I applied for jobs. You know what happened."

Jamal sighed. "You let one injury ruin you."

Carter shook his head. "All I'm saying is, it would've been nice for her to be there for me."

Jamal smirked. "You just needed your ego stroked. You a trip, bruh. She stayed there with you the whole-time bro. her dreams went to millions you should've went with her and helped with the company."

Carter looked down at the floor, his jaw tightening.

What Jamal was saying yeah, it stung. Not just because it was bold, but because it was true. Slick, but true. The words hit harder than he wanted to admit, pressing against parts of him he was trying to ignore.

But the decision had already been made.

He had to stick with it now.

So instead of responding, Carter just paused—silent, still, and staring at the ground

Jamal laughed and said, "Man all I can do is support you and your wishes but be careful with that. They say Tracy is low down, and you're leaving a total package for a hood thang."

Carter shakes his head and says, "Go to work," before walking away. Jamal yells back, "Something you should've done with Mya, but you're definitely about to have to do with Tracy." Carter needed to choose his happiness, and that's something Mya wasn't giving him. Mya was the most beautiful girl walking, while Tracy had the body men wanted.

Chapter 9
LET IT FADE

The night had finally fallen, and Mya locked the door to the boutique behind her, feeling a mix of exhaustion and relief. The day had been long, filled with customers and the soft hum of business moving forward. London had helped keep things light, but inside, Mya's heart still carried the weight of everything that had happened in the past few days.

She walked to her car, keys in hand, scanning the street for somewhere to grab a quick bite. The thought of cooking or going home to an empty house made her stomach twist, so she drove aimlessly, letting the night air clear her head. As she rounded the corner, she saw a small, dimly lit sign that read, The Blue Chat Lounge. The jazz club looked like a relic of the past, something timeless and inviting. It was a place that felt familiar even though she'd never stepped foot in it before.

Mya parked the car, took a deep breath, and walked inside. The moment she crossed the threshold, the smooth, velvety sound of a saxophone greeted her, setting a quiet, soothing mood. She approached the host stand, where a woman with a warm smile greeted her.

"Table for one?" the hostess asked.

Mya nodded, feeling a little self-conscious but determined. "Yes, please."

The hostess led her to a booth by the window, where she could see the streetlights outside and hear the faint hum of the music. The atmosphere was comforting, a gentle escape from the chaos in her mind.

Once seated, Mya ordered her food. A simple meal of salmon and vegetables, and then sat back, letting the smooth jazz wash over her. Being alone wasn't something she was used to, but she was hoping for something different when she got home. She realized how much she had been neglecting herself in the past few months. Always putting her marriage and business before her own peace of mind. I guess I need to get used to this, she thought quietly to herself, staring at the glass of water in her hand.

The music swirled around her, and she let herself sink into the rhythm of it. Just as she was about to take another sip of her water, she saw a familiar face in the doorway.

Damon.

Her breath caught in her throat as he spotted her and started walking towards her table with a confident stride. He was wearing light-washed jeans and a crisp shirt, his haircut sharp and clean, looking like he just got a fresh cut. Mya blinked, not sure if she was imagining things. When he got closer and their eyes met, she couldn't help the surprise that shot through her.

"What are you doing here?" Mya asked, voice a little softer than she intended.

Damon gave her a knowing look. "This is my go to food spot, Every Monday I slide through to get some grub. What you doing eating alone?"

Mya tilted her head, slightly skeptical. "You didn't hear the news?" She let out a bitter laugh, half-shaking her head. "Everybody's talking about it."

Damon's expression shifted, and he hesitated for a moment. Then he looked down, fiddling with his fingers before finally meeting her eyes. "Yeah... I heard. I always knew Carter was a mess, but I never thought he'd go that low," he said quietly.

Mya stared at him for a long beat, her fingers still curled around the glass of water. She felt like she had so much to say. She wasn't sure how to say it, or even if she should. Finally, she put her glass down, her voice barely above a whisper. "I mean, I should've known. Everyone knew but me, I guess. He never wanted to come up to New York. He barely even answered or returned my calls... what did I expect?"

Damon didn't flinch at her bitterness. Instead, he sat down in the booth and let out a sigh. "You expected him to be a man. To be responsible and, to be there for his wife. You expected him to live up to his vows. Marriage is a covenant, and that's why I'm in no rush to get into one."

His words struck her like a physical blow, but they were also a relief. Mya had been feeling so much anger, confusion, and doubt that she didn't even know where to start untangling it all. Yet, Damon's perspective, though blunt, gave her a moment of clarity.

She closed her eyes for a second, taking in his words, letting them sink into her. When she opened them again, she looked at him, her expression softer but still guarded. "How long has this place been here?" she asked, trying to change the subject, if only to steady herself.

Damon knew what she was doing he just went with it. "This place been here for about a year now. Otis's son opened it up. The food's pretty good too, if you're into that soul food type vibe."

Before Mya could say anything else, her waiter came to deliver her food. A steaming plate of perfectly cooked salmon and vegetables, along with a side of mashed potatoes that smelled like comfort itself.

"Thanks," Mya said with a small smile, but her attention was already starting to drift back to Damon. He looked at her for a moment longer, then stood up.

"Well, I'll let you get to it. I'm still in the neighborhood. If you need anything, just hit me up." He gave her a nod before turning to walk out, looking as good as ever in his light-washed jeans and crisp shirt.

Mya watched him go, the sound of the jazz band filling the silence between them. She couldn't deny the way her heart skipped a beat, but at the same time she couldn't ignore the guilt that tugged at her. I don't need to be looking at no men while I'm still married, she reminded herself sternly.

CHAPTER 10
CARTER

Carter gripped the door handle of his old, rusted pickup truck and pulled it open with a grunt. The sun was beginning to set, casting a golden hue across the street as he parked in front of the house he once shared with Mya. A familiar ache tugged at his chest as he noticed the empty driveway. Mya's car wasn't there.

He rushed inside, quickly grabbing the last of his things—clothes, a few belongings, and the remnants of a life he had abandoned. He shoved everything into the back of his truck, slamming the door with a finality that felt hollow. This was it. No turning back.

As he pulled out of the driveway, Carter felt a rush of relief. Tracy's apartment was his next stop, and while part of him dreaded it, he knew that this was where he had to be now.

When Carter arrived at Tracy's apartment, he was immediately hit with a sharp, unpleasant smell that made his stomach churn. Tracy was in the kitchen, yelling at her kids to sit down at the table, the noise making the place feel even smaller than it was.

"Hey, baby," Tracy greeted him, giving him a kiss on the cheek. "I see you got the rest of your stuff. Was wifey there?"

Carter froze for a moment, the words catching in his throat. He didn't know how to answer her. Finally, he muttered, "Nah, she wasn't there. Actually, I didn't even get a chance to talk to her."

Tracy smirked she turned to the stove and stirred whatever disaster she had cooking.

Carter pulled out a chair from the half-broken dinner table and sank into it with a sigh. "I got to find me a job now I guess," he said, his voice heavy with the realization of how much he had let everything slip.

Tracy didn't miss a beat. "You sure do baby, but I know you will do anything for your family, and we are going to be here supporting you." she said, "You know I can't work. I've got these kids to take care of and if I go work it's going to mess with my check."

Carter rubbed his temple, feeling the headache setting in. "I need to run to the pharmacy," he muttered, hoping to avoid any further discussion about his financial mess.

As he walked out the door, he was hit by the reality that his truck was almost on empty. He slammed the door in frustration and leaned against the rusted metal, trying to catch his breath. How did I get here?

The weight of it all was suffocating. Carter started walking to the corner store, hoping to clear his head for a few minutes, but as he turned the corner, he froze. There, standing in front of the store, was the pastor.

"Carter, is that you, man?" The pastor's voice rang out, friendly but laced with a knowing tone.

Carter looked over, his eyebrows shifting in surprise. "Yeah, it's me. What's good, Pastor?"

The pastor walked toward him, holding a receipt in his hand. "Man, it's good to see you. How you been?"

Carter dropped his gaze to the sidewalk. "I'm makin' it," he muttered, though it didn't feel true. "You know, just... tryin' to survive."

The pastor studied him for a moment, his expression thoughtful. "You seem a little stressed, son. That new woman isn't what she seemed, huh?"

Carter winced. The pastor's words hit close to home. His instincts told him to shut down, but he couldn't ignore the truth.

He shifted uncomfortably; hands stuffed deep into his pockets. "I'm not really trying to get into this. It's done now. It wasn't planned it just happened. I got caught up in the moment." His voice trailed off, unable to fully justify his actions.

The pastor shook his head gently. "That wasn't just a moment, Carter. That was more than that. You built a whole new life man. You hurt a good woman, and now you have to live with that. Mya... she's a good woman and she will be okay."

Carter's jaw clenched, and he stepped back. His chest tightened with frustration. "I'm a good man, too. You don't know what it's been like man. She left me for her dream she didn't think about me. A couple of texts and phone calls and pictures of her living it up, and I was just supposed to follow her? No one ever asked me what I wanted. No one cared about that."

The pastor sighed, his voice calm but firm. "Carter, I understand your pain. She was wrong, and as a team she was supposed to treat you like her partner. However, you're being selfish. Instead of trying to compete with your wife, you should've been there, building with her. Marriage is a partnership, not a competition. You don't get the spotlight all the time, you both share it equally."

Carter felt the sting of those words. He had never truly considered it that way. Everybody had their own opinion about him, but nobody acknowledges what she did. He thought of Mya, working so hard to make her dreams come true, and he'd been too focused on himself to support her. He was too busy feeling sorry for himself to notice that she needed him by her side.

"Well now, I'm stuck, so I just got to stick with it. Tracy ain't that bad either. Nobody perfect." Carter said, exhaling loudly. "I'm figuring out how I'm going to support Tracy, and all these kids shoot."

The pastor's face hardened. "Wait a minute. You didn't have a job when you were with Mya?" The disbelief in his voice made Carter flinch.

"Do you think that little thing you're dealing with is going to let you live off her? You're crazy, Carter, yeah you better figure it out haha" the pastor added sharply.

"Now, Pastor—" Carter began, but the pastor cut him off.

"Nah Carter. I'm serious what were you thinking man. Never mind I know, you were thinking about that thang in your pants not with your heart—you know what, get on your knees and lift your hands."

Carter was taken aback, confused, "What you got going on pastor?" Slowly, he sank to his knees in the middle of the parking lot, not caring who saw. He lifted his hands toward the sky, feeling exposed, vulnerable, and lost.

"Jesus, I'm sorry," the pastor said, his voice quiet but powerful. "You heard me – repeat what I said."

Carter echoed the pastor's words, his voice rough with suspicion. "Jesus, I'm sorry..."

The pastor paused, then smacked him lightly on the back of the head. "For being stupid!" he said with a chuckle. Carter blinked, then stood up, his face a mix of surprise and frustration.

The pastor stepped back and sighed. "I'm kidding, Listen, man, this is not just about you. You must submit to God and make things right with your wife. This mess you're in, only God can fix it. You've got to let Him take control, and if you decide that you don't want to be with her anymore then you need to do it the right way."

Carter stood up, wiping the dirt from his pants. "Yeah, I know. I get it."

The pastor slapped him on the shoulder. "Don't forget what we talked about, and remember, it's never too late to come back to Jesus. Jesus is the main thing and without him you are nothing."

Carter watched the pastor walk away, his words sinking in like a seed buried deep in his chest. Maybe it wasn't too late, but he can't just drop Tracy she had his son.

As Carter walked back to Tracy's apartment, he felt a strange sense of clarity. The apartment was quiet when he walked in, the kids nowhere in sight. He collapsed onto the old, worn-out couch, the memories of his past mistakes flooding him. The life he had built—such as it was—felt so far away now.

He buried his face in his hands, overwhelmed by the weight of his decisions.

Chapter 11
REBALANCE

The weekend had rolled around, and Mya was determined to reclaim her life. The house, now quiet and empty. The laughter, the arguments, the dreams they had once shared it all echoed through the rooms like a distant memory. Today, she was ready to make this house her own, not a place of sorrow, but a place of peace, strength, and new beginnings.

Mya had gospel music blasting through the speakers, the uplifting melodies filling the space as she swept and cleaned. She scrubbed away the remnants of the past, washing away the hurt and the heartbreak. It felt therapeutic, the steady rhythm of the cleaning, the cleansing of her soul as she scrubbed every corner. Each stroke of the mop felt like a prayer.

Just as she was about to start rearranging the furniture, there was a knock at the door.

She paused, she wasn't expecting anyone. Then, a familiar voice echoed from the other side.

"Mya, open up!"

Mya recognizing her brother's voice. She quickly opened the door, and there stood Trevor, looking as laid-back as always. His eyes scanned the room, taking in the changes she was making to the space.

"I see somebody's getting back to themselves," he said, his gaze sweeping over the newly organized room, and the subtle changes Mya had already started making.

Mya couldn't help but smile. "No choice, no need to keep staying down" she replied.

He raised an eyebrow, taking in the scene. "Exactly. That was a bum you were carrying... I don't know why you let him hold you back this long."

Mya chuckled, rolling her eyes. "Exactly. I was carrying him, and he couldn't hold it down for a little bit."

Trevor laughed. "Exactly, couldn't handle a woman getting it, but wanted to lay on his back while you were working. I'm proud of you tho – for not staying down to long" he said with a grin, always the first to tease, but also always the first to have her back.

Mya turned back toward the couch, sinking into it with a sigh of relief. She felt lighter already, as if some of the weight had been lifted just by starting the process of taking back control. "You know what? I'm about to call the girls over. It's time for us to have a good time. He wasn't the only reason I came back."

Trevor shot her a playful glance. "That right there is what I'm talking about, boss up on em big sis."

Mya grabbed her phone and began texting her best friends, letting them know it was time for a girl's night. The energy in the room shifted as she typed, the excitement bubbling in her chest. She looked up from her phone and noticed Trevor lounging in the chair across from her.

"Guess who I saw the other day?" she said, raising an eyebrow.

Trevor leaned back, looking intrigued. "Who?"

"Damon Fears," Mya replied with a small smile.

"Damon? Oh yeah, I heard D's doing good. He's got his own packaging company, right?" Trevor said, nodding, a bit of surprise and curiosity in his tone.

"Yep, he's doing really well," Mya said. "It got me thinking. Why don't you work with him? You know, get something stable for a change."

Trevor grimaced at the suggestion, shaking his head. "Nah, I'm not trying to be a delivery man, Mya. I don't want to be driving trucks around for a living."

Mya's eyes narrowed in playful disbelief. "Trevor, you need a job. You can't keep running around these streets. You'll end up dead or in jail. I'm serious. You need something more than this."

Trevor's expression softened. "I'm not like that anymore, Mya. Seriously, I'm trying to get into construction, Something real. You know, real man work."

Mya raised an eyebrow, unconvinced. "Construction? You know you don't know nothing about no hammer and nails."

Trevor grinned, leaning forward to make his case. "Sis, I'm serious. I really do. I've been looking into it, and I've got a few leads. It's what I want to do."

Mya stared at him, her skepticism clear on her face.

Trevor held up his phone, a wide grin spreading across his face. "See? They're calling me right now. It's about the construction lead."

Mya's expression softened, the concern in her eyes giving way to a hint of pride. "Okay, I see you. Let's see how it goes then."

Trevor stood up, brushing his pants off. "Let me get out of here. I've got to take this call. I'll let you know what happens, but I'll catch you later."

"Alright, thank you for checking on me," Mya said as he turned to leave. "If you don't get this job, don't give up, keep going!"

TINA

Tina sat in the dim light of her apartment, which had seen better days. The walls were cracked, the furniture mismatched, and the air smelled like a mix of old food and stale memories. However, she didn't care.

Caleb, her energetic little boy, ran through the apartment with a ball in his hands. "Mama, where's daddy? Why he never comes home?"

Tina paused, a soft smile tugging at her lips. She watched Caleb for a moment, the innocence in his eyes making her heart ache. "Mommy's here baby, Go play. As long as I'm here we good" she said, her voice filled with as much assurance as she could muster, even if it was a lie.

She watched him run off, the sound of his laughter echoing down the hallway. Tina sighed deeply, her mind wandering to Ray Ray—the man who had promised her everything and delivered nothing. She reached for her phone and, without thinking too much, dialed his number. The phone rang once, twice, and then, to her surprise, he picked up.

"I knew I was going to hear from you again baby mama" Ray Ray's voice sounded as cocky and unbothered as ever.

Tina took a deep breath, steeling herself for what she had to say. "Ray, your kids are needing you now. You might not want to do right by me, but don't become a deadbeat father."

There was a brief pause on the other end of the line, and then Ray Ray spoke, his voice dripping with defensiveness. "Let me stop you right there. I'm a good daddy, Tina."

Tina's patience snapped. "A good daddy? Then come and see your kids, Ray! They need you, and you're too busy out there living your life like we don't even exist. So don't call yourself a 'good daddy' if you're not showing up. Your son over here asking why you aren't coming home. You can come get him we don't have to have no dealings"

The line went quiet for a moment, and Tina hung up, frustration bubbling up inside her. She turned away from the phone and walked toward the kitchen. She wasn't going to beg him. Not anymore. Caleb needed a father who actually cared, not one who showed up when it was convenient.

She grabbed her phone again, opening the group chat with Mya and Diana. After a few moments of hesitation, Tina typed, *"Yes, I need this night."*

Before she could put the phone down, she scrolled through social media and stopped when she noticed something new, Chase had followed her. She raised an eyebrow, a small smirk playing on her lips. "Well, well, well, look at that."

Tina clicked on his profile, her eyes scanning his pictures. He had that charming, confident energy that she found irresistible—smart, successful, with a touch of that rough around-the-edges charisma. This one fine brown brother here, she thought to herself, her mind beginning to wander.

Without overthinking, Tina followed him back. Just as she leaned against the counter, her phone buzzed with a notification. She glanced down. Chase is calling on the gram.

Her heart skipped a beat. She quickly grabbed the water bottle from the counter, taking a deep swig to steady herself. What was this man calling her for? She hesitated for a second but then put on her best seductive smile and answered the phone, making her voice as smooth and confident as possible.

"Hey, Chase," she purred, pretending like she wasn't caught off guard. "What's up?"

"Hey, Tina," he replied, his deep voice sending a warm shiver down her spine. "Just wanted to see how you're doing. You had me rolling at the party."

Tina's breath caught, but she quickly masked it with a playful laugh. "I'm good, just chilling with my son."

They both laughed, and just like that, the conversation flowed easily. They talked for hours about everything from their childhoods to their experiences with love, their jobs, and everything in between. Tina felt heard. She felt seen. Chase had a way of making her feel special, something she hadn't realized she craved until now.

Before they knew it, the conversation had stretched well past two hours.

Chase's voice softened a bit as the conversation wound down. "So, after your girl's night tonight, you wanna grab some dinner? Maybe hit up that live music restaurant vibe you told me about?"

Tina felt a smile spread across her face. "I'd love that," she said, her voice soft and flirtatious.

"Just hit me when you get from your girls' night. I can't wait to see you again." Chase said with a grin.

As they hung up, Tina sat down on the couch, feeling a new sense of excitement bubble inside her. Hoping that this wasn't just a one-off fling.

She looked around her apartment, the clutter and brokenness that used to fill her with frustration now feeling like an afterthought.

Tina really didn't know how Mya was going to react, but that's none of her business. At the end of the day, she and Chase were both single and she didn't owe mya no explanation.

DIANA

Diana's heels clicked sharply on the polished marble floors of the law office as she finished up the final touches on a big case. It had been a long week of reviewing documents, holding meetings, and keeping everything together for her clients. As a top attorney, Diana was used to being the one everyone leaned on colleagues, clients, even friends.

Her assistant, Emily, came in with a stack of papers, placing them on Diana's desk with a warm smile. "That's the last of it for today. You've been working non-stop. You sure you don't want me to handle the rest?"

Diana shook her head. "Thanks, but I've got it. I can't let anything slip now." She flashed a tight smile, one that didn't quite reach her eyes.

Emily nodded, sensing the exhaustion behind Diana's usual composed facade. "Alright, well, I'll head out. Don't stay too late, okay?"

"Promise," Diana said, her voice softening a bit. As Emily exited, Diana leaned back in her chair and let out a long sigh, allowing herself a moment of reprieve.

She glanced at her phone, seeing several messages come through. Most were work-related, but one caught her eye, an invite from Mya to a girls' night at her place. Diana paused for a moment, looking at the message. She had been so wrapped up in everyone else's drama that she hadn't made time for herself lately.

She smugged typed back, "I'll be there" She hit send and set her phone back down, hoping that this wasn't another night of hearing Tina and Mya problems, but just something fun and relaxing.

Diana had always been the strong one. She was the friend who kept everything together. Mya with her emotional upheavals, Tina with her baby daddy problems, and everyone depended on her guidance and support. Who took care of her? Who listened when she was falling apart, when she felt stretched too thin.

With a sigh, Diana gathered her things and made her way out of the office. She stepped into her new luxury car, the leather seats enveloping her as she started the engine and drove through the bustling streets. As she turned onto the highway leading to her house in the suburbs, she received another text, this time from Tina.

"Hey girl, can you pick me up for tonight? I'll be ready in about 20 minutes. My mama watching the kids, so she needs my car".

Diana looked at the message. Feeling here it goes I must go out my way again for them. She typed "Of course, I'll be there."

Her phone buzzed again as she made her way toward home, and she saw the message from her sister. It was a routine message, checking in on her. Diana quickly typed back, telling her everything was fine, and she'd be home soon. As much as she loved her family, sometimes they didn't get it. They didn't understand the pressure of her job, the constant balancing act.

When Diana arrived at her house, she walked into the kitchen. She opened the fridge and grabbed a bottle of Coke, pouring herself a glass over ice. The coldness of the drink felt refreshing, grounding.

She kicked off her heels and slipped into something more comfortable. A soft pair of yoga pants and a cozy oversized sweater. Diana felt the weight of the day lift slightly as she changed into clothes that made her feel more like herself.

Then, she made the call she had been putting off all day her grandfather. She dialed the number, letting it ring a few times before he answered, his voice cracking slightly with age but filled with warmth.

"Diana, baby, is everything okay?"

"I'm good, Grandpa. Just wanted to check in and let you know I'm heading out tonight, but I'll be back later. So, I won't see you after your bingo night."

There was a pause on the other end of the line, followed by a small chuckle. "You're heading out? Since when does my granddaughter leave the house for something other than church or work? Who's the guy?"

Diana chuckled softly, trying to hide the exhaustion in her voice. "There is no guy grandpa, it's just me and Tina and Mya."

Her grandfather's voice softened, "Well, alright, baby. Be careful and have fun."

"I will, Grandpa. I promise."

After they finished the call, Diana sat in silence for a moment.

As Diana pulled up to Tina's apartment, Tina stepped out onto the small porch. She opened the passenger door and slid into Diana's car, looking around before buckling her seatbelt. The moment Tina sat down; both of their heads snapped to the right when they saw Carter walking out of the apartment building five doors down.

"Carter" They both said looking at each other.

Diana's heart sank as she watched him, strut like he owned the world.

Tina let out an exaggerated gasp, clapping her hands together. "Ahhh heck naahhh—what in the world is he doing over here?!"

Diana couldn't help but exhale a little laugh, shaking her head as she watched him walk towards his truck. Of course he was here, Diana thought. Of course, he'd show his face.

Tina's nostrils flared. "Girl, I ought to go over there and punch him right in his face. Just bam! Give him a piece of my mind, maybe even knock that smirk off his face for good."

"No, no, no," Diana quickly responded, shaking her head with wide eyes. "That is not a good idea at all."

Tina huffed in annoyance, crossing her arms as she watched Carter from the corner of her eye. She wasn't backing down so easily. "I swear, this man doesn't know how to leave well enough alone."

Just then, Diana shifted in her seat, trying to get a better view. "Hold up—who is that walking out with him?" she asked, narrowing her eyes. A figure appeared behind Carter. Tracy. His new woman. She waved at him as he climbed into his truck, completely oblivious to the fact that two women were watching his every move from the car across the street.

"Tracy?" Diana muttered in disbelief. "How could he be right next to you Tina, and you didn't know at all?" She couldn't even hide the surprise and frustration in her voice.

Tina clenched her jaw, shaking her head slowly. "Girl, that's how dirty some men are. They will do all that mess right in your face—right under your nose."

Both women slid down in their seats, trying their best to keep a low profile, hoping Carter wouldn't spot them from across the street. They didn't need him to see them, especially with Tracy so close. When Carter finally got in his truck and drove off.

Diana leaned back in her seat. "Lord, if that's not a hot mess…"

Tina glanced over at her, squinting. "He probably been hanging with Ray Ray. I bet you that's where he's been. They both don't know how to act. Tracy been with Ray and now Carter."

Diana let out a soft groan. "Dang, Ray Ray still ain't got his act together, huh?" she said, shaking her head in disappointment.

Tina threw her hands up. "Nope, I'm starting to think he likes playing with me, making me look crazy. I swear, every time I let him back in, he does this mess. I'm over it. I'm moving on.
What's that phrase you say? I'm putting it in the Lord's hands."

Diana glanced at Tina, a mix of shock and concern crossing her face. "Girl, you say that all the time."

Tina stared out of the window, her gaze distant but resolute. "Girl I'm serious. I'm done. This time, I'm really done."

Diana sat in silence for a beat. Tina never said something so sure. Diana finally shook her head with a soft laugh, impressed with Tina's newfound determination. "Wow girl you serious, I'm proud of you."

Tina gave a half smile, her usual sassiness back in full force. "I've gotta be. Ain't no man gonna have me out here looking like a fool again."

The two women continued their drive, the atmosphere lit from the music. Soon enough, they pulled up to Mya's house.

Trevor was sitting on the porch, casually talking on his phone. He nodded as the women walked up to the door. Tina shouted out, "Hey, Trevor!" as they approached.

"Yo, what's good?" he greeted them, throwing up a peace sign.

"Hey Trev, how are you?" Diana asked, giving him a quick look. He seemed to be doing better since their breakup.

"Yeah, I'm good," Trevor said, grinning and holding up his phone. "Just handling some business. Y'all go ahead in."

Mya greeted them with open arms when they stepped inside. "Hey, y'all, come on in!" Her smile was as bright as ever, and her positive energy radiated through the room.

Tina and Diana exchanged a quick look, eyebrows raised in unison. "Is everything okay, Mya?" Diana asked, her concern evident in her voice.

Mya's smile never wavered, but she gave them a small nod. "Yeah, everything's fine. Why?"

Tina raised an eyebrow and threw her hands up dramatically. "Lord, she delusional. This girl—crazy!"

Mya burst out laughing, waving her hand dismissively. "You know what? I'm fine. Just not letting that mess hold me down."

CHAPTER 12
GIRLS NIGHT

The laughter and chatter filled the air as the girls settled on the couch in Mya's freshly rejuvenated living room, a space that felt so much more like home now. It had been a while since they'd all been together like this without the hustle, without the distractions of their individual lives, it was just them.

Mya glanced over at Tina, who was poking at her food, not really eating. "Girl, why aren't you eating? What's wrong?" Mya said with a raised eyebrow, a teasing smile on her face.

Tina laughed, shaking her head as she readjusted her legs on the couch. "I guess I'll say, y'all I'm going out on a date tonight" She dropped the bomb like it was nothing, but the sudden excitement in her voice made both Mya and Diana turn their heads in disbelief.

"Wait—a date?" Mya echoed, her eyes wide. "With who?"

Tina grinned, looking from Mya to Diana, who were both equally intrigued. "I can't say, yet I'm not ready to release that yet not until I know what it is" she said nonchalantly.

The two of them looked at each other in surprise and then back at Tina, both of them grinning ear to ear. "Oh, you were for real about dropping Ray Ray. Well, we are happy for you." Diana exclaimed.

Tina paused, adjusting her legs again as if making herself more comfortable with the news.

Mya's eyes widened. "Wait. Hold up. What about Ray Ray?" she asked, genuinely curious.

Tina smirked and shrugged. "Exactly. What about him."

The room erupted in laughter as Mya leaned back onto the floor, her arms outstretched on the carpet. "I missed this y'all" she said softly. "Seriously, I didn't have this in New York. Everything was just so fast. I was so focused. I barely had time for myself, let alone for you guys."

Diana nodded in understanding, her tone softening. "I get it. I've been so caught up in work and trying to make a name for myself, running the law firm, taking care of my family... It's not easy at all."

Mya rubbed Diana's arm for comfort. "I know you've been carrying so much, D, but I'm proud of all you've done girl."

Diana smiled, grateful for the small moment of peace. "I've been telling myself that for years now. It's hard when you're expected to always be the one to hold it together. Sometimes, I just want to be vulnerable too. I want to feel like I can lean on someone."

Mya gave her a small smile. "You can, we've always got each other."

There was a long pause, and then Mya spoke again. Her voice a little quieter. "When I came back, I didn't know how it would turn out. I didn't know if I'd fit back in with y'all, or if this place was still home. Now, knowing that I've got you two, I'm glad I came back. Even though it's been a pitfall after pitfall... being with you guys is all I need."

Tina nodded in agreement, her expression softening. "Girl, we are always going to be good. No matter what happens, we're in this together. I was so worried, you know? I thought I didn't amount to anything. I let that mess with Ray Ray ruin my life, and worse, it started affecting my kids."

Mya sat up from the floor, her eyes full of empathy. "You've always amounted to something, Tina. Don't forget that. You're stronger than you know. Now you do the most, but you mean well. Jesus brought this and us altogether for a reason."

Diana smiled, her eyes softening as she looked at her friend. "Mya, I'm just glad you're finding your way back to Jesus, girl. You know that's what's been missing."

Tina chuckled softly, shaking her head. "Girl, you're talking about Jesus like you're a preacher or something."

Mya laughed. "Honestly, I was so far from myself it wasn't even funny. I was so caught up in what I wanted and being selfish. I wasn't available for anybody, and I'm pretty sure that's what ruined my marriage. Then watching my grandma go through so much. It made me not want to be in the faith. Everything that was going on and the only person I could lean on is the Lord."

Diana reached over and placed a hand on Mya's shoulder. "Well, let me be the first to say, welcome back to the kingdom."

Diana glanced over at Mya, curiosity in her eyes. "So… you and Chase never had a moment?"

Mya scrunched up her face. "Heck no. I wouldn't even think of it."

"Why not?" Diana asked, genuinely intrigued.

"I just never been interested in him," Mya said, shaking her head. "He's not my type. Too… well put together for me. You know I like a lil hood."

Tina burst into laughter. "Girl, a well put together man is way better than a bum or a hood man any day I had both. Honey, I need a well put together man."

Mya and Diana laughed with her, nodding in agreement.

"I don't know," Mya said, shrugging. "I guess I didn't want to mess up the friendship we have. We also do business together, and a relationship would just complicate too many things."

Tina grinned, doing her best not to release about her date. "Chase is fine though."

"Girl, so fine," Diana added, fanning herself playfully.

Mya laughed again. "I mean, if y'all are into that. He doesn't look bad, but I only look at him like a brother. I used to think he was into me, but I friend-zoned that quick."

Tina tried to keep her face neutral, but the slight expression she made was one she quickly tried to hide.

Chapter 13
TRYING LOVE AGAIN

Tina finally made it home, her heart racing with excitement as she thought about her date with Chase. She quickly told her mama she would be back after her date

She quickly got ready, opting for a sleek, all-tan dress that hugged her curves just enough to feel confident and very revealing. She wanted to show that she had class, that she was ready for something real. She looked in the mirror, making sure everything was perfect, and smiled at her reflection. She was nervous, but she was also excited.

When she arrived at the restaurant, she saw Chase standing at the entrance, waiting for her. As soon as he saw her, he stood up, his eyes lighted up. "Wow," he said, his voice warm and sincere. "You look... absolutely beautiful."

Tina blushed, a shy smile tugging at her lips. "Thank you. You look really good yourself."

They exchanged pleasantries and sat down at their table. The evening flowed smoothly as they ordered their food, enjoyed the music, and talked about everything and nothing. Tina's nerves started to ease as they talked, the conversation flowing naturally, like they'd known each other for much longer.

After dinner, Chase surprised her by asking her to dance. She hesitated at first, glancing around at the empty dance floor. "What you mean… no one else is dancing, all these people are going to be looking at us." She said, her voice laced with fear.

Chase smiled warmly. "I don't mind, the way you are looking they should look. Come on, I promise it won't be as bad as you think."

Tina hesitated, but then she allowed herself to trust him. She stood up, her heart racing as he took her hand, leading her to the dance floor. The music swirled around them, the gentle melody pulling her in. For a moment, it felt like it was just the two of them—like nothing else mattered.

She leaned her head gently on his shoulder, the scent of his baccarat cologne soothing her. She felt safe. She felt wanted. If that was Ray they would've went back home and had a good bliss night, but she is doing things the right way for once.

The song came to an end, and the crowd erupted in applause, signaling the end of their dance. They pulled away slowly, both of them slightly breathless. Tina adjusted her hair, still trying to compose herself.

When she looked up, she found herself locking eyes with Chase. The chemistry between them was undeniable.

"Let me walk you out," he said softly, his voice full of warmth.

Tina smiled, feeling a rush of down her body. Taking his hand, and they walked out of the restaurant together.

Mya

Mya hummed softly as she cleaned up the remnants of the girls' night, the soulful strains of Tasha Cobbs Leonard filling the room. She wiped down the counter, her movements rhythmic, almost meditative. The house, though still in transition, was starting to feel like home again.

A knock echoed.

Who could that be? She said to herself. When she opened the door, she was pleasantly surprised to see First Lady, her bright smile lighting up the doorway.

"Praise the Lord, Mya!" First Lady greeted her with a voice full of warmth. She stepped inside with an air of joy that felt like sunlight after a storm. "I came to pick up my dress and, of course, to check on you! I hope you're doing okay, honey. You look amazing and the house is definitely cleaner than last!"

Mya smiled, "Thank you, First Lady. I'm just getting back to myself, you know? Slowly but surely."

"I'm glad to see it, baby," she said, glancing around the house, taking in the changes with approval. "It looks like you're making it through. You've got to keep it that way, okay? Don't let the devil knock you off your course again."

Mya nodded, feeling the weight of First Lady's words. She had a quiet strength about her that Mya admired.

Then, the conversation shifted.

Mya's brow furrowed as she asked, "I can't believe Carter has kids..."

First Lady paused, looking at her with a raised eyebrow. "Girl, those ain't his kids."

Mya blinked in confusion. "Wait, hold up? Carter said they were."

First Lady chuckled softly, shaking her head. "Nope, Tracy's been putting those kids off on everybody. She's been lying to Carter telling him they were his, and he's just been going along with it."

Mya sat down slowly, processing the shock of it all.

"Wait, so he doesn't even know?"

"Nope," First Lady said with a smirk. "He's just been the fool in the situation, believing whatever Tracy told him. It's a mess, honey. Carter did this right here to himself."

Mya sat in stunned silence, trying to reconcile the man she thought she knew with the man First Lady was describing. Her mind was racing, trying to make sense of everything.

First Lady gave her a knowing look grabbing her dress. "I've got to go now. You take care of yourself, okay? I hope to see you at the ball next week. It'll do you some good to get out there and be around some good people."

Mya nodded absently, still processing what First Lady had just told her. "I'll try. Thanks for checking in."

As First Lady left, Mya closed the door softly behind her, her thoughts a whirlwind.

She sat down at the table. She needed to pray. Her heart was heavy, but she continued praying. The words flowed more easily as she poured her heart out to God. She prayed heaven down for Carter's restoration, and maybe her own too.

Another knock echoed through the house.

Mya stood, wiping her face quickly. When she opened it, her breath was instantly caught in her throat.

There he was. Carter.

Her pulse quickened, and her heart seemed to sink into her stomach. It had been days since she last saw him, and she had worked so hard to get herself together. She thought she was ready to move on but seeing him at the door pulled at every emotional thread she had been trying to keep tied.

"Mya... can I come inside?" Carter asked quietly.

Her lips parted, but for a moment, no words came out. She stood frozen in the doorway; caught between the woman she had been and the woman she was becoming. Finally, after a long pause, she stepped aside, and Carter entered without another word.

He looked around the room, noting the changes, the tidiness that was now in place. "I see you've changed things around here. It looks nice," he said soft rubbing his hands together.

Mya didn't respond immediately. Instead, she crossed her arms and gave him a steady, serious look. "What is it, Carter? What do you want?"

Carter looked down at the floor, as if gathering the courage to say what he needed to say. "Mya... I just want to say I'm sorry. You didn't deserve any of this. You were good to me. You were too good to me."

Mya's eyes narrowed, her frustration creeping back up. "Too good? More than good!" she said, the words tasting bitter in her mouth.

He nodded, "Yes, too good. I've been so selfish, only thinking about myself. I wasn't thinking about you. I wasn't thinking about us. Now, I see that I've messed everything up."

His voice wavered slightly, and Mya's heart broke a little. She knew Carter was hurting, but could she trust him again?

"I've been praying, baby," Carter continued, his eyes earnest. "I've been praying for a chance to make it right. I need us back. I can't keep living like this, separated from you. Please, Mya... please let me prove to you that I can change."

Mya lowered her gaze, her mind a swirl of emotions. She had prayed for him to come back. Prayed for this moment, but was she truly ready to open her heart again?

"I prayed and prayed for you to come back, Carter," Mya said softly, her voice barely above a whisper. "I was broken, and there's so much that's happened. So much that needs to change."

Carter took a small step toward her, reaching out as if to bridge the gap between them. "I'll change, Mya. I'll do whatever it takes. I'll be the man you need me to be. I've been selfish, but I'm ready now. I want to lead our family. I want to build something with you, something that lasts. Please find it in your heart to forgive me."

Tears welled in Mya's eyes, but she fought them back, trying to maintain control. God says forgive. She remembered the words. Remembering her prayers of healing for him, but could she really forgive?

Before she could respond, the knock at the door interrupted them again.

Mya wiped her eyes quickly. She opened the door, and standing there was the social worker. She was accompanied by two children, both of whom were quietly observing their surroundings.

"We found a match for you, Mya and Carter," the social worker said kindly. "Here is James and Olivia. They'd prefer to stay together, and we wanted to see if now's a good time for them to come?"

Carter looked at Mya, a look of understanding in his eyes. "Perfect timing," he said softly, nodding toward the kids.

Mya stepped aside to let the children and the social worker in, but she couldn't ignore the gnawing feeling in her chest. She had agreed to foster, but now, with Carter not in the picture she didn't know what to think.

Mya pulled Carter to the side, her expression firm. "Carter, we need to talk about this." Her voice low but sharp. "Right now, is not a good time."

Carter exhaled, and his frustration evident. "Mya, what better time than now? With everything going on, and all my mess ups. God sending we us not one but two kids. This is God showing us right here."

Mya turned away from him, her eyes flickering toward the social worker, who had been quietly observing the tension between them.

"If this isn't a stable home," the social worker said carefully, "I can take the kids back."

Carter's breath hitched, and he quickly shook his head. "This is a stable home. I promise."

Mya forced a smile, but Carter could see right through it. Carter knew she was lying. He knew their marriage was hanging by a thread, blown apart by a decision he thought he wanted, only to realize too late that he didn't.

The social worker studied them for a moment before nodding. "Alright. Well, if you need anything, call me. I know these kids are going to be in great hands."

Mya smiled and turned and walked toward the bedroom where the kids were going to be staying. Pushing the door open, the social worker softened her voice and looked toward the kids. "If you two need anything, you can call me, okay?"

The children nodded, looking uncertain.

The social worker gave them a reassuring smile before stepping back. "I'll be doing check-ups, so I'll see you all soon. Goodnight."

As the social worker left, Mya led the kids to a room, doing her best to smile, but inside, she felt torn. She turned back to Carter once they were settled.

"I need more time, Carter," Mya said quietly. "I'm not ready to jump back into this. You need time to figure some things out one minute your gone and now you're back? It doesn't work like that. I think you should sleep where you've been sleeping. I need space to think, and I don't think these kids need to be wrapped up in our stuff."

Carter looked like he was going to say something, but then he just nodded. "I know you think I need more time, but I have made my mind up. if I'm not with you, then I don't want nobody. However, I'll respect that. I love you, Mya."

Mya's heart tightened in her chest. "I love you too, Carter."

She closed the door softly behind him as he exited the house, the weight of the decision still heavy on her shoulders. She fought back the tears, knowing the road ahead was uncertain, but this was her path to healing.

She wasn't sure where it would lead.

Carter stepped out of the house, the night air hitting him like a wake-up call. He paused on the porch, glancing back at the door.

He knew exactly what he was walking into, but what stung more was knowing that no matter what he said, Mya had to make her own decision, and it wasn't his job to control it.

She always thought she could do it all alone, shutting him out, making decisions like he was just an afterthought. The controlling individual she'd always been.

A bitter scoff escaped him as he turned away, making his way to his truck. He yanked the door open and slid inside, gripping the steering wheel like it was the only thing keeping him together.

Chapter 14
Grandma ways

Mya woke up early, the sunlight creeping through the blinds and catching the gleam of her red-bottom heels sitting at the foot of her bed. She stretched, then slipped into her best outfit—a sleek dress, a fitted blazer, and her signature Gucci brooch. Every detail was perfect, from the polished heels to the crisp lines of her jacket. She was ready for church.

Olivia and James were next on her list. She walked into their room, already anticipating the chaos of getting them dressed. James was sprawled across the couch, half-eaten cereal in his hand, eyes glued to the TV. Olivia, the younger one, was still under the covers, her hair a tangled mess.

"James, time to get moving, we are going to church so come on." Mya said, her tone both gentle and firm. She picked out a white button-down shirt and some khakis for James, and a pretty pink dress for Olivia. She managed to tame Olivia's hair into a neat ponytail, though it wasn't perfect.

"Sorry I couldn't do your hair better, Liv" Mya said, trying to reassure her.

Olivia smiled shyly, but didn't say a word. Meanwhile, James dropped his cereal on the coffee table and slouched back into the couch.

Mya eyed him. "Hey, James, let's try to keep the eating in the kitchen so we don't get bugs."

James shot her a sideways glance, mouth full. "I've lived with plenty of bugs. They're not so bad."

Mya frowned. "I don't do bugs. So, in here we won't have bugs."

Olivia gave James a cautious look, but he got up heading to the kitchen. Though he was the older sibling, he knew better than to mess things up for them.

"I'll be right back, and when I get back James, I need you to be dressed" Mya said. She slipped out the door, leaving the kids in the house.

Crossing the streets to Trevor's place, her mind already bracing for the mess that awaited. As she approached the porch, her lips twisted in disgust at the unkempt space. She pounded on the door, then yelled, "Trevor! Open up!" No answer.

With a sigh, she spotted the spare key in the windowsill. "This boy never learns," she muttered, grabbing it. She unlocked the door, stepping inside with a mix of frustration and familiarity. The place looked unchanged same old ratty furniture, the same ugly green walls that seemed to be peeling with age.

The smell. Mya wrinkled her nose. "What is that? I know he is not using that flat screen in a house that look like this. Grandma's probably turning in her grave."

She made her way to the bedroom, her heels clicking on the hardwood floor. "Trevor, I know you heard me knocking at the door."

Trevor startled, pulling the covers over his head like a child caught red-handed. "What are you doing in here? When you are going back to New York" His voice was groggy but defensive.

"I have the spare key now," Mya said, yanking the covers off. "Get up. We have to go to church."

Trevor groaned and rubbed his eyes. "Woman, are you crazy? I haven't been to church in ages. Jesus is in my heart."

Mya threw her hands up in exasperation. "Well, let's get Him in your day, too. Come on, I need you to meet the kids."

He frowned, sitting up and throwing the blanket off. He wore nothing but shorts and a tank top, his du-rag still on his head.

"What kids?" he asked, looking around the room like he was still half asleep.

Mya's eyes narrowed. "You really need to clean up in here."

He waved her off. "Are you not listening to me? What kids? I know you don't have Carter kids?"

Mya sighed, her patience wearing thin. "The social worker came by yesterday. She brought me two beautiful kids to foster." She paused, watching his expression shift. "Carter was there—apologizing. Trying to come back."

Trevor froze, his eyes narrowing as he processed the news. "Hold on, hold on. Carter came by… apologizing?"

Mya nodded. "Exactly what I said. He came by, apologized, and tried to make things right."

Trevor propped himself up on the fireplace mantle, still not convinced. "So, did you tell the social worker you and him were done?"

"I tried," Mya said, "Carter stopped me and accepted them before I could explain. I couldn't just turn them around" Trevor's jaw tightened. "You're not going back to that punk, right?"

Mya hesitated, the weight of the question settling between them. "I haven't figured it out yet."

Trevor's voice grew louder. "Mya, that dude humiliated you in front of everyone. How do you think I'm supposed to just let that slide? You go back to him, and now all of a sudden, there's kids involved? He is trying to re-trap you. He only coming back because he realized he don't have money without you."

Mya walked up to him, her tone calm but firm. "I'm figuring it out, Trevor. When I got married, I made a vow to love, for better or worse. I take that seriously. I know it hurt you, heck it hurt me too, but I made a covenant. Through all the mess, Carter wasn't all bad." In reality he was just all she knew. Her eyes met his eyes, her voice softening. "Now, will you come on and get ready for church? Let's do this right."

Trevor studied her, trying to gauge her sincerity. Deep down, he knew she was holding on to Carter for reasons beyond love for comfort, for the familiarity of what they had. He couldn't let go of the feeling that something was still pulling her back.

He walked to his room and dressed in a polo shirt and jeans; his gun holstered at his side. When he came out, Mya spotted it immediately. "Trevor, take that mess off your side."

He raised an eyebrow. "Girl, I'm not stepping out the door without it. This is the peacemaker."

Mya rolled her eyes. "We're going to church, not a shootout."

Trevor locked the door behind them ignoring Mya. As they headed across the street. Mya introduced him to Olivia and James as "Uncle Trevor," and they all piled into Mya's Mercedes, making their way to church.

When they arrived, the church was bumping. They sat with Diana, who was already tapping her foot to the gospel music that filled the sanctuary. The atmosphere was electric voices raised and the congregation alive with energy.

Then Damon walked in, sharp in a well-tailored suit, his fresh waves glinting under the church lights. Mya bit her lip, eyes lingering on him as he approached the front of the church. "That man knows he looks good in a suit, and he's serving the Lord".

Diana leaned over, whispering, "Keep those thoughts in your head, girl."

Mya chuckled softly. "Girl, I thought I was."

When the service wrapped up, Damon made his way over to Trevor. "My boy Trev! It's good to see you in the house of the Lord."

Trevor grinned, slapping Damon on the shoulder. "Yeah, one of the Lord's new servants woke me up."

Damon laughed. "Well, I hope they keep waking you up."

After they dapped each other up, Damon turned to Mya. "Hey, Mya, aren't you looking beautiful? Good to see you in the house of the Lord."

Mya smiled. "Thank you, you're looking nice in your fitted suit. I see you!"

Damon leaned in closer to her looking around "So when do I get the honor to take you out?"

Mya regretting what she was about to say, but it was the right thing to do "Right now isn't a good time, I'm still married"

She hated to admit it, but she didn't want to miss seeing him, but what about Carter. The way Damon smiled at her, the way he looked at her like she was the only woman in the room, made her feel things she hadn't felt in a long time. Things Carter haven't made her feel, but she still had to remember that she is still married. She couldn't do what Carter was doing to her and start forming feelings for Damon.

"That's right," Damon said with a teasing smile.

As Mya walked to the car, where Trevor and the kids were waiting, Diana called out to her. "It was so good seeing you in church sis, but I have one question. Who are those kids?"

Mya smiled, a knowing glint in her eyes. "Girl, I'll tell you real soon. I gotta go, but we are going to talk."

Diana narrowed her eyes, then pulled out her phone. "Mhm."

Mya pulled into Trevor driveway, the engine purring softly as she brought the car to a stop. She glanced at the porch to see a woman on Trevor porch.

"Who's that?" Mya asked, her voice tinged with curiosity.

Trevor, who had just gotten out of the car, paused for a moment and looked over. "That's crazy Nina," he said, his tone laced with resignation.

Mya couldn't help but shake her head and laugh. "Boy, you keep some mess and you keep a woman." She rolled her eyes, but the amusement was clear on her face.

Trevor threw his hands up dramatically as he got out of the car. "Don't come over here with all that! I just gave my life to the Lord, and now the devil's sitting on my front porch!"

Mya heard the playful outrage in his voice as she started driving off, shaking her head with a smile. "He something else" she muttered under her breath as she made her way back to the house.

As she pulled into the driveway of her own home, she cut the car's engine and turned around to face the kids.

"So, what did you two think about church?" she asked, trying to keep her voice light but also genuinely curious.

Olivia glanced at James before responding, as if silently asking for his permission. Mya noticed the hesitation and gave Olivia a warm smile. "It's okay to talk, Liv," she reassured her.

Olivia's gives a small but genuine. "I think it was good. It was my first time being in a church," she said softly, her voice carrying a quiet sense of hope.

Mya's heart softened. "I'm glad you liked it, sweetie," she said, her voice full of warmth.

Turning her attention to James, she asked, "How about you, James? What did you think?"

James didn't answer right away. His eyes were fixed on the outside world, his face unreadable. After a long beat, he just shrugged his shoulders rising with a subtle gesture that felt like a wall going up between them.

Mya's smile faltered slightly. She was used to his silence. "Oh, wow. Okay" she said softly, not wanting to press him further.

Without saying another word, James swung open the door and climbed out of the car, his movements quick and deliberate.

Olivia looked at Mya, her expression understanding. "Don't worry about him. We've just been through so much. He doesn't really know when we're safe yet," she said, her voice steady despite the sadness in her eyes.

Mya nodded, feeling the weight of Olivia's words settle in her heart. She could see the concern in the girl. "Well I promise you both are safe with me," Mya said softly, her voice filled with empathy. "I understand more than you know."

Olivia gave her a small, almost tired smile before getting out of the car. She walked over to where James stood on the porch.

Mya sat in the car for a moment, watching them. Her heart was heavy, but she took a slow breath and said a quiet prayer.

"Lord, you're going to have to help me with this," she whispered to herself. She wasn't sure how it was all going to work.

DIANA

Diana finally pulled into her driveway. As soon as she walked through the door, she grabbed her phone, eager to spill some tea. She dialed Tina's number and waited for her to pick up.

The phone rang a few times before Tina finally answered, her voice sleepy but sharp. "Girl, what is it? I was just about to take a nap!" she grumbled.

Diana didn't waste a second. "Girl, guess what? Mya and Trevor came to church today."

Tina still half sleep. Sat up in her bed her interest somewhat piqued. "That's good for her. You know she trying to get herself together since Carter. Hold up Trevor? So, you was in church with your Ex? I'm surprised that church didn't catch on fire with Trevor being in there" she said, sitting up straight.

Diana chuckled. "Girl I'm serious, and that's not even the craziest part."

Tina raised an eyebrow. "The craziest stuff happen in church I need to start going. Girl what?"

Diana paused for a dramatic effect. "She had two kids with her. A little boy and a little girl."

Tina froze for a second, her bonnet slipping off her head. She narrowed her eyes at the phone, her voice flat. "Hold up. Kids? What do you mean, kids? Who had kids? Them better not be that girl and Carter kids. Mya would do some dumb stuff like that."

Diana leaned back in her chair, enjoying the suspense. "I don't know, girl. She said she's gonna tell us more later, but she just showed up with them, and I'm telling you it was so awkward. Then Damon came up trying to take her out. Like dang D she aint even divorced yet".

Tina's eyes went wide, and she sat up even straighter. "Girl, you're lying! Damon? Talking about mid-size fine Damon? I thought he was married. Girl, I need to know more!" She was already making mental notes. "Let me start doing some undercover work. Mya's always up to something sneaky. Then have the nerve to be taking care of Carter kids?"

Before Diana could respond, her sister Molly's voice rang out from the other room. "Di! I need you!"

Diana sighed, holding the phone away for a second. "I don't think those were Carter kids, but you right the way Mya gets with Carter there is no telling what that man can trick her into doing, but I gotta go, girl. Molly's being dramatic again. I'll call you back."

"Yeah, alright, but you better fill me in later!" Tina hung up quickly.

Diana threw the phone on the bed as Molly came into the room, looking all sweet and innocent.

"What Molly?" Diana asked, her tone already bracing for whatever ridiculousness her sister was about to bring.

Molly said to her, wearing her usual expression. "Sis, I need to borrow some money."

Diana's eyebrows shot up. "What do I look like to you, a walking ATM? You still haven't paid me back that last loan."

Molly pouted, "Come on, sis. Just a little bit... I swear I'll pay you back this time."

Diana stared at her for a moment, not buying it. "How much do you need?" she asked, already knowing she wasn't going to give it to her anyway.

Molly looked to the side. "I need $1,400."

Diana blinked, then burst out laughing. "Girl, what do you need with that kind of money?"

Molly casually leaned over, coming closer to Diana. "Well, me and Tyquez are starting a slushie business. His aunt gave him her old equipment, and we need the upfront money for supplies and all that."

Diana scrunched her face, looking both confused and skeptical. "A slushie business? You've officially lost it. I'm not investing in that. What do you think this is, Shark Tank?"

Molly's eyes went wide. "Really? You're not gonna help me? I'm your sister at least you could do is try to help. You know Tyquez is a good guy, and we could make this work!"

Diana, still shaking her head, looked at her with disbelief. "Girl, get out. I can't believe you came over here to ask me for money instead of going to Tyquez's aunt, who's the one who gave him the equipment in the first place."

Molly rolled her eyes. "That's sad D, you could at least try to invest we are blood." She walked out of the room, her footsteps heavy with annoyance.

Diana stared at the screen for a moment before switching to her dating app. She scrolled through profiles, her face growing increasingly irritated. "Dang, why won't I match with anybody but these weird-looking nerds?" she muttered aloud, clicking away at the screen.

Just then, Molly's head popped back into the room, her voice dripping with mischief. "how are you stuck-up but have the nerve to be searching for a man on a site" she said, a sly grin spreading across her face.

Diana didn't miss a beat. She grabbed the nearest pillow and flung it at her sister. "GET OUT, Molly!" she screamed, laughing despite herself.

Molly ducked her laugh echoing down the hallway as Diana slumped back onto the bed, grabbing her phone once more.

Hearing a knock at the door.

Diana's voice echoed down the hallway, groaning slightly. "What is it now, ugh."

Opening the door, she froze, her eyes narrowing. "Ray? What are you doing over here? Tina isn't here."

Ray Ray stood on her doorstep, his face full of anxiety. His usual swagger was gone, replaced with something she'd never seen in him before. "Di," he said, his voice low, "I'm sorry to pop up like this, but I didn't know what else to do. I knew Tina wasn't gonna help me with this, but I really need your help"

Diana frowned. "I mean can you blame her for not wanting to help you with anything." she murmured under her breath, crossing her arms.

Ray Ray looked at her, a slick smirk crossing his face. "Chill this is serious Di."

His smile faded quickly, replaced by a more serious look. "Look, someone's trying to frame me for something I didn't do, and I need your help. Bad. Please." His voice cracked slightly as he spoke, raw and pleading.

Diana's stomach tightened. "Ray, what have you gotten yourself into?" she asked, scanning his face for any signs of exaggeration. She didn't see that she saw fear. Real fear.

Ray Ray glanced over his shoulder, looking down the street as if the world itself might be watching him. "I don't know who, but they've got evidence fake evidence. They're setting me up, D. I'm telling you. I need your help."

Diana hesitated for a moment. She knew Ray Ray, and she knew when he was in trouble. This wasn't some street hustle or a petty issue this was bigger. She couldn't just turn him away. "You're asking for a lot, Ray. You know Tina is my best friend, but I'll do the best I can." she said softly, crossing her arms again as she leaned against the doorframe. " Just... just tell me what's really going on."

He nodded quickly, relief washing over his face. "Thank you, Di. I'll explain everything. Just… let me get back with you.

I have to go handle something really quick."

He rushed off to a beat-up car parked across the street, the engine sputtering as he drove away, disappearing into the late afternoon sun.

Diana closed the door she pulled out her phone and texted Tina. *Girl, call me back when you can. We need to talk.*

Chapter 15
New Horizon

Chase stepped into his New York apartment. Excited to be back home. The apartment was quiet—eerily so, but as soon as he walked through the door, Mya's dog came bounding toward him, tail wagging furiously.

"Hey, buddy," Chase said, crouching down to ruffle the dog's fur. The animal nuzzled into his hand as if nothing had changed. He allowed himself a moment of solace in the simple.

He didn't know what to make of Mya anymore. He was drawn to her there was no denying that. She was polished, successful, and confident in ways that made most men second guess themselves. The way she carried herself, how everything about her seemed effortlessly perfect, intimidated him, in a way. Deep down, he knew she was out of his league. Moreso, she didn't really see him the way that he saw her.

It wasn't just Mya that had him tangled. It was Tina.

Chase exhaled slowly as he flopped onto the couch, the dog curling up at his feet. Tina was nothing like Mya. Where Mya was measured, Tina was bold. Loud. Vibrant. There was never a dull moment with her. She was unapologetically herself—flaws and all and that was refreshing. Even if it occasionally pushed him to the edge of his comfort zone.

He remembered their date clearly, the way she made him laugh uncontrollably, how her energy was contagious. She was beautiful too, in a way that was easy to see but hard to explain. Her light skin, her deep brown eyes that sparkled when she spoke. Everything about her made him want to lean in, to know more, to dive deeper.

As much as he was drawn to her, a part of him couldn't shake the fear of heartbreak. He had been down that road before. The risk of putting his heart on the line again… it was almost too much.

He ran his hand over his face, trying to shake off the confusion. If he was being honest with himself, he didn't want to miss out on either one of them. The truth was, he didn't know what he wanted. Maybe he was too scared to figure it out.

Chase reached for his phone he hesitated before unlocking it. He opened the messages app and stared at Tina's name. His thumb hovered over the keyboard before he typed out a simple, neutral text *Hey.*

He stared at the message for a long time. He sighed and hit send,

Meanwhile, Tina was in her apartment, scrolling through her phone aimlessly. With a day of rest. She kept glancing at the screen, waiting for any kind of notification from Chase. She had been patient to patient, honestly, but the truth was, she couldn't stop thinking about him. She'd replayed their date in her mind a thousand times, wondering if he felt the same spark. He'd been distant since then, leaving her unsure of what to make of it. When she heard her phone buzz, her heart skipped a beat.

She grabbed her phone, quickly opening the message. Her eyes widened in surprise.

Hey.

"Just... hey?" Tina scoffed to herself, a mixture of excitement and irritation bubbling up inside her. This man really sent me a 'hey'? She stared at the text for a moment. She knew it was nothing, but the small part of her that still held out hope felt the tiny thrill of finally hearing from him.

She immediately began typing her response but stopped herself. Don't overdo it, she thought, chewing her lip as she tried to keep her cool. He probably wasn't expecting much.

She hesitated. Maybe a simple "hello" would work. Then she thought—nah, she wasn't about to start playing these games. So, she typed instead Hey stranger and hit send with a sly grin.

Then she set the phone down on the kitchen counter feeling like she just did something. Walking to her room with a deep breath, trying not to obsess over her reply. I'm not doing this, she told herself, even as she was already counting the seconds in her head, wondering how long it would take for him to respond.

As Chase sat back on the couch, his mind wandered again, but this time, it was to Tina. He knew he had a lot to figure out, but for now, he was content with the simplest of interactions.

Even as his phone buzzed with Tina's message. Hey stranger. He chuckled softly at her playful tone.

Chase sat back, his fingers hovered over the keyboard as he composed his message. I'm sorry, I was on my flight and just got back. So, I guess that means you were thinking about me?

He added a winking emoji just for a little flair.

Tina was walking back into the kitchen when she heard the familiar ping of her phone. She grabbed it, already knowing it was Chase, and smiled as she read his message. Flirting? She bit her lip, feeling that familiar excitement rise in her chest. A sly grin played across her face as she quickly typed a response, maybe so...aww, I hate I don't get to see you again.

She hit send before she could talk herself out of it. She was already imagining his face when he read her words.

Chase's phone buzzed again, and he grinned as he saw her reply. You hate it? He couldn't help himself. His fingers flew over the keys. Well, you can always come to New York...

Tina stared at her phone, laughing softly to herself. She knew he was playing around, but part of her was like, could I? She called Diana before she could think about it too much.

Diana picked up on the second ring, her voice full of excitement. Girl, I've been trying to get in touch with you!

Tina smirked. "What's up, D?"

"Girl," Diana practically shouted," how about Ray Ray shows up at my door asking for help? He said someone trying to frame him, girl, what he got going on?"

Tina rolled her eyes and leaned against the counter, letting out a small chuckle. "That sounds like a Ray Ray problem, not mine. There ain't no telling what he has been doing.".

Diana laughed. "You a mess. Do you think I should help him, though?"

Tina's twisted her mouth. "Girl, if you want to, help him. I'm over that situation. He can handle his own stuff. He doesn't need me anymore and I don't need him."

Diana surprised, "This new man must be good for you."

Tina raised an eyebrow. "Girl, you have no idea. Enough about Ray, my new man wants me to come to New

York."

There was a beat of silence on the other end of the line, then Diana's voice broke in, almost a little too excited, "Wait, WHAT? She practically shouted. Girl, I'm coming! Who is it? And when are we going?"

Tina's smile deepened, but she wasn't about to spill the beans yet. "Girl, I'm not ready to say just yet, not until I actually know what this is."

Diana didn't hesitate. "Mhm, I guess so..." She paused, then grinned. "It must be something if he wants you to come to New York. Girl, you better say, as long as you're paying, I'm coming. Tell him to make sure there's enough for me to come too!"

Tina shook her head, laughing. "I just can't believe he want me to come out. Girl, I have never been outside of the country, but I'll let you know when it's time to pack your bags."

They shared a laugh before Diana said, "Alright, girl. I'm gonna let you go. Call me later, okay?"

"Of course," Tina said, "Talk soon."

Chapter 16
Them Kids

Mya was strolling through the mall with Olivia and James trying to make the best out of the Sunday evening. Olivia was practically bouncing off the walls with excitement, tugging at Mya's sleeve every few seconds.

As they approached the entrance of the store, Mya glanced over at James, who was walking a few steps behind them. His eyes scanned the area warily, his posture stiff, like he was ready for something to happen at any moment. Mya could tell he wasn't entirely comfortable.

"James, are you okay?" she asked, her voice soft, but still laced with concern.

James looked up, startled, and stammered, "Yeah I'm okay."

Mya wasn't entirely convinced, but she decided to let it slide for now. Maybe it was just his way of handling new situations. She gave him a small smile and gently nudged him towards the store.

As soon as they walked inside, Olivia couldn't contain herself any longer. "I've never been shopping before!" she exclaimed, her voice ringing with excitement. She dashed off towards the racks, grabbing at clothes like it was Christmas morning.

Mya chuckled, but her eyes quickly flicked back to James. He was standing off to the side, arms folded across his chest, eyes still darting around, watching Olivia but not moving much himself.

She made her way over to him, her voice gentle, "James, don't you want to go around and look? There's lots of stuff here."

He shrugged, his eyes still following Olivia. "I'm okay with the clothes I have. You can just focus on Olivia."

Mya paused for a moment, her heart tightening a little at the way James was holding himself back. She could tell he wasn't used to this having someone care enough to pay attention to what he needed. She wasn't about to let him slip away.

"I have enough for you both," she said, her tone firm but loving. "Come on over here with me and let's find you something. You deserve it."

At first, James hesitated, then slowly walked over to where Mya was standing by a rack of jeans. She held up a pair and smiled, "How about these?"

James' face lit up a little as he saw them. "I've been wanting jeans like these," he said, his voice growing a bit more animated. "Some of the guys at school has some, and they look so dope."

Mya's heart swelled with warmth. She knew this was a moment.. "Well, let's see if they have your size," she said, grinning.

James looked down at the jeans and then quickly put them back. "Uh… I don't know my size, it's okay I don't have to get any today" he muttered, his voice trailing off.

Mya smiled softly, squatting down to his level. "That's okay. Let's figure it out together, you don't have to give up so quick James." she said, her voice reassuring. She started flipping through the racks, picking out a few pairs in different sizes and showing them to him.

After a few moments of searching, they found the perfect fit. James stood a little taller. "These are perfect," he said quietly, his eyes sparkling.

"Great choice," Mya said, smiling. "Let's get them."

They made their way to the checkout, with Olivia happily showing off a few new dresses she had picked out. Mya loaded everything onto the counter, but when the total flashed on the screen—$500. James' eyes went wide. He immediately started reaching for the clothes he liked the least.

"We can put some stuff back that's too much money," he said, his voice low and uncertain.

Mya shook her head gently laughing. She placed a hand on his shoulder. "James, I got this. You be the kid, baby. I'm the parent," she said firmly but lovingly.

For a split second, James just stood there, blinking. He hadn't heard those words before— "I got this." It wasn't just a promise; it was reassurance. For the first time in a long while, he felt safe, like he could be a kid without worrying about everything around him.

He stepped back, a shy smile tugging at the corner of his mouth. His shoulders relaxed, and for the first time in a while, he felt something close to peace.

Olivia, still smiling, leaned up against the counter and whispered to him, "Don't worry, James. Mya got it."

Mya finished paying and handing the bags to the kids. She gave James a quick glance.

As they walked out of the store, Mya couldn't help but feel a shift between them. James wasn't just a boy who had been dropped into her life for no reason. He was a kid who was starting to experience safety. That meant everything to Mya.

Mya finally pulls into the driveway, the engine of her car rumbling to a stop. She notices a familiar truck parked in front of the house, and her stomach tightens when she sees Carter leaning against it, arms in his pockets, waiting.

James immediately tenses up beside her, his whole body going rigid. He mutters, "Who is that?" as his eyes narrow.

Mya takes a deep breath, trying to keep calm. "It's okay, James. Go inside and grab your stuff. Open the door for your sister," she says softly, yet firmly.

James hesitates, looking back eyes locking on Carter, but Mya gives him a look that pushed him towards the house.

Mya walked toward Carter, each step measured, controlled. He looks up at her as she approaches, his face softening. "Hey, Mya," he says, his voice low.

"Hey, Carter," she replies, her words cool but not unkind.

He watched her for a beat, as if trying to gauge her mood, then finally says, "How have you been?"

Mya pauses for a second, her tone guarded. "I've been alright, you?"

Carter's eyes search hers, and he steps a little closer. "I'd be better if we could come back together Mya."

Mya stands her ground, not allowing his words to weaken her. "You know right now that's not possible." She's proud of herself. She's holding firm, keeping her boundaries even though a part of her—the part that used to love him deeply wants to cave.

Carter looks at her, frustration creeping into his voice. "How are the kids?" he asks, trying to steer the conversation toward something that might tug at her heart.

"They're fine," Mya answers quickly. "How are your kids?"

Carter falters for a moment. There's a flicker of discomfort in his eyes. "Let's not go there" he mutters, clearly avoiding the topic.

Mya stands tall. "If not now, then when, Carter?"

For a moment, Carter just stood there, staring at her, his chest rising and falling. Then, his voice cracks slightly, "Mya, I'm seriously sorry. I messed up I know it, but I love you. I love you with everything in me, baby."

Mya watches him plead with her, his words stirring something inside her. She began to remember the good times—the way his hazel eyes would soften when he looked at her, the warmth of his butterscotch skin, the vein in his neck popping out when he was passionate. All of it rushing back.

"If you loved me, Carter," she says, her voice steady, "you wouldn't have gone out and created a new reality without me. Now you expect me to just take you back and accept all of that."

Carter looked defeated. "We need to talk about the adoption then" he says, a hint of desperation in his voice.

Mya crosses her arms. "let's talk about it."

Carter tries to argue, his words losing some of their power. "Maybe we need to hold off. I'm not in the right place right now nor am I in the home so that's not providing a stable life for the kids."

Mya's gaze hardens. "Wow... really." Mya scoffs. "I'm not letting them go back into the system. I'll do whatever it takes to keep them with me. You've got some nerve." She begins walking away without looking back.

Carter stands there, watching her. Shakes his head and gets in his vehicle, driving off without another word.

Mya's heart is heavy as she walked into the house. James' voice breaks through her emotion.

"I was listening," he says, his voice small. "Why won't you just take the man back? We're finally comfortable here. We are not about to go back to that place!"

Mya's eyes immediately soften."James," she whispers, her voice thick with emotion, "You two aren't going anywhere. I will do any and everything to protect you and Olivia. You're mine now, and I'll fight for you both."

Tears slip from James' eyes, and Mya holds him tighter, wishing she could give him everything he needed to feel safe. She pulls back, wiping her own tears away. "Go put your new clothes up, baby. There is nothing for you or Olivia need to worry about."

James nods, heading to the room him and Olivia share, but Mya is left standing in the living room, feeling more uncertain than ever. She sinks down on the couch and closes her eyes. "God, please... give me the wisdom and strength to protect these kids."

She lets the silence wash over her, but then her phone rings, snapping her out of her thoughts. She glances at the screen and sees Chase's name.

"Hey Mya," his voice comes through the line warm, but casual. "What've you been up to?"

Mya leans back into the couch, letting out a breath. "Just trying to survive over here. How's New York? Oh, how I miss it so much!"

Chase chuckles. "It's nice, crowded, and loud as always. But hey, I've got a question for you."

Mya raises an eyebrow. "Uh-oh, what's wrong? Is my dog getting on your nerves?"

"Nah, nah," Chase laughs. "Everything's fine. I just wanted to let you know that Tina and I have been talking. I know she is your friend, so I didn't want it to blindside you."

Mya's eyebrows knit together. "Oh ok, that's good. I'm glad to have you in the friend group."

"No, I mean... we're talking, talking, like getting to know each other" Chase continues, his voice a little hesitant. "We went on a date before I left."

Mya's heart skips a beat, but she forced herself to stay calm. "Oh, wow. Uh - how did that happen?"

Chase hesitated before answering. "It just kind of happened, and I wanted to make sure you were okay with it. I know we work together and she's your best friend. I don't want to overstep, but I'm feeling her."

Mya pauses, her mind spinning. She hadn't thought much about Chase in that way but hearing that he was with Tina... kind of stung. She cleared her throat. "Well, I guess there isn't nothing for me to say. Other than you know, just take care of my friend. Whatever happens don't let it get between our friendship and money."

Chase felt a pang of disappointment but tries to hide it. He knows it's not going anywhere with Mya, so he might as well make it work with Tina.

Chapter 17
The Dream

London is standing behind the counter, looking frazzled as she watches customer after customer flood into the shop. She glances at her phone and sighs. "Mya hasn't been here in days, I haven't even heard from her" she mutters under her breath, feeling the weight of the chaos. "I didn't sign up for this."

Just then, the door swings open, and Trevor strolls in, grinning. "This place booming, ain't it? I need to be getting some of this money" he says, his voice loud and playful, drawing attention.

London shoots him a look, trying to hide her frustration. "Exactly it's booming and I'm the only worker. Have you heard from Mya?"

Trevor shrugs, unbothered, before walking closer to her. "I talked to her couple of minutes ago what's up?"

London sighs again, clearly stressed. "Well, someone needs to tell her to come help out at her store."

Trevor looks a little taken aback. "Let me step out here and call her." He says while walking out.

"Hold on! Hold on!" she calls out, but Trevor's already halfway to the door.

A few minutes pass, and Trevor comes back inside. "She's on her way. I can't believe she left you in here" he says with a smirk shaking his head.

London glares at him. "Well, I don't think she expected it to be this much, but if you could help me out in the meantime" She trails off, not needing to say more.

Trevor walked over to the counter, clearly ready to pitch in. Just then, the door opens again, and Damon walks in, holding a package.

Trevor grins and waves. "What's up, bro?" he says as he approaches Damon.

Damon nods, a friendly smile spreading across his face. "What's good man, just dropping off some packages," he says, handing them to London.

London gestures toward a nearby table. "You can sit them over there. I'll get to it in a second."

Trevor, ever the eager helper, smacks Damon on the shoulder. "Let me help you out, bro."

"Aight, bro. Come on then."

As the guys begin sorting through the packages, Mya finally walks in, looking apologetic. "I'm so sorry about this," she says, clearly out of breath. "Where do you need me?"

London just looks at her with a raised eyebrow, half relieved and half-annoyed. "At the register, please."

Damon comes back in seeing Mya.

"What's up, Mya, I didn't know you were here. It's usually just London" Damon calls out.

Mya looks up, a smile tugging at her lips. " Yeah, she has been holding it down. I just got here, and we are packed out."

Damon nods, his eyes lingering on her for a moment. "That's a good thing" he says with a smile noticing how busy she was before turning to leave. "I'll catch you later."

Mya watches him walk out, her gaze lingering a little longer than she means to. The man is good-looking, no doubt about it. He's hardworking—something about that appeals to her, especially in this environment where things are chaotic.

Before she can snap back to reality, a customer at the counter clears their throat. "Excuse me, are you going to help me, or just watch him walk out?" they ask, slightly annoyed.

Mya blinks, snapping back to attention. "Oh, my bad sorry. Yes, let me help you!" she says, offering a sheepish grin.

The customer smirks, clearly not bothered by the brief distraction, and Mya quickly moves to ring them up, still a little flustered by the moment.

The store had finally calmed down. Mya took a breath. The shelves were nearly bare, the last few customers had trickled out, and she found herself standing amidst the empty space, looking around at what she had built.

London, who had been running around like a whirlwind all day. "I can't believe how crazy this has been," she said, sinking into a nearby chair.

Mya walked over, feeling the weight of the exhaustion. "I am so, so sorry, London," she said, her voice sincere. "I brought you here with me and just put all this on you."

London sighed. "Yeah, it's been non-stop. I need a break." She looked at Mya, her expression softening.

Mya nodded. "I'm sorry. You've been doing more than your share." She gave a small smile, trying to lighten the mood. "Why don't you take the rest of the day off?

I've got it from here."

"You sure?"

"Yeah," Mya said, walking toward the counter. "Go home, relax, take a breather. I've got it covered."

London stood up, to go grab her things. "Alright, well, if you need me, you know where I'm at." She headed for the back room, gathering her jacket and purse.

As London stepped out, Mya walked slowly through the store, taking in the shelves, the merchandise, and the work still left to do. She couldn't help but reflect on how much had changed. From opening the store to dealing with her broken marriage, the surprise of getting two new kids, and the constant juggling life had taken so many unexpected turns.

Her thoughts drifted to God. She felt the weight of everything on her shoulders, and yet, there was a stillness inside her, a knowing that she wasn't doing this alone. She walked toward the window, her hands resting on the cool surface as she looked out over the street. With a sigh, she prayed.

"Lord," she said, "thank You for this place. Thank You for bringing me this far, for everything I've been through and everything still to come. I ask You to open new doors, Lord, bless this business, and guide me. Help me create something that honors You. Send people to help, people who are dedicated to Your mission. I need Your wisdom and Your grace more than ever, Lord."

The door bell chimed, and Trevor stepped inside, his usual confident stride cutting through the stillness. He glanced around the shop, looking pleased but also a little curious. "Did I just hear my sister praying?" he asked, teasing but with a hint of admiration.

Mya let out a small laugh, surprised at how natural it felt to have him pop in like this. "Yes, you did," she said, shaking her head slightly "I just needed to thank God, with all that has happened he's still been good."

Trevor folded his arms, leaning against the counter. He looked at her with a knowing gaze. "I've watched you get crushed and come back to God, Mya."

Mya smiled softly, her heartwarming at his words. "Honestly, Trevor, it's not me at all. It's really the grace of God. If it were up to me alone, I wouldn't have made it. He's truly been carrying me."

Trevor nodded slowly, a little quiet for a moment, as if reflecting on her words. "I see that. You're stronger than I ever gave you credit for." He stepped closer, a little more serious now. "You know, sometimes I wonder if I'm doing enough. If I'm doing what I'm supposed to."

Mya's expression softened, her eyes meeting his. "You've got a good heart, Trevor. Don't think you have to carry everything on your own either. We're all in this together. You and me, now the kids... we're family."

Trevor looked at her for a long moment, his face softening with the quiet understanding between them. "You're right. I guess we'll just keep going, huh?"

Mya smiled, a little tired but determined. "Yeah. Keep going."

Chapter 18

Courage

Mya locked the door behind her and took a slow breath as she stepped outside the store, the cool air of the evening brushing across her skin. Her day had been full—chaotic, tiring, but now, with the shop finally closed, it felt like she could take a moment to breathe. Just as she was about to head to her car, a familiar voice called out from across the street.

"Mya Jean?"

Mya froze. She hadn't expected to run into anyone right now, let alone someone who knew her full name. She turned to see Miss Penny, her old neighbor, standing on the sidewalk with a wide grin on her face. Her eyes lit up when she saw Mya.

"Miss Penny!" Mya said, equally surprised, but smiling as she walked over to her. "Oh my goodness, I didn't expect to see you out here."

"Girl, you look amazing!" Miss Penny exclaimed, taking Mya in from head to toe. "It's so good to see you, baby. How you been? You back from that big ol' city?"

Mya laughed, feeling a warmth in her chest at Miss Penny's enthusiastic tone. "Yes, ma'am. I'm back. I've been good, just, you know, getting things in order."

"Well, I remember your grandmother telling all of us about how you were gonna take over the world in that ole clothing industry," Miss Penny said, shaking her head in amusement. "She was so proud of you, honey. She probably smiling down on you right now." Mya laughs and say, "Fashion

Industry". Miss penny sharply say, "Don't interrupt me you know I forget stuff."

All Mya could do was laugh. Gloria had been such a big part of her life. "Yeah, I miss her every day," Mya said softly.

Miss Penny smiled sympathetically. "I know you do, baby. You're doing the work she knew you'd do, taking care of things and that ole brother of yours is a hot mess. He was supposed to come cut my grass I haven't seen him yet."

Mya laughed "I can't believe him, I'm going to let him know."

Miss Penny paused, her eyes scanning the street as the sun began to dip behind the horizon. "You tell him! Well, I've gotta get on over to the grocery store. It's getting late, and I don't want you out here by yourself. You better head on home before someone snatch you up, now," she warned with a wink.

Mya smiled; her spirits lifted by Miss Penny's warmth. "I will, I will. You be careful too, Miss Penny."

"I always am, baby, they know not to mess with me." she said before heading off in the direction of the corner store.

Mya watched her for a moment before turning and heading back to her car, a little smile lingering on her face. It felt good to reconnect with her roots, to remember the people who helped shape her.

As Mya pulled into her driveway and stepped out of the car, the house felt unusually quiet. She walked inside, calling out softly, "James? Olivia?" No response.

She headed toward the kids' rooms, her heart beginning to race as she knocked on their doors, checking to see if they were there. Empty. She called their names again, louder this time, panic starting to creep into her chest. Where were they?

Then she noticed a faint light on the back porch. Her heart skipped. Without another thought, Mya hurried to the back of the house.

When she stepped outside, she found both James and Olivia sitting quietly on the porch, their backs turned to her, staring out into the yard. The look on their faces was both solemn and uncertain. Mya's breath caught as she stepped closer.

"Hey," she said softly, walking toward them. "What are y'all doing out here? Is everything okay?"

They both looked up at her, their eyes filled with a quiet sadness that Mya wasn't sure how to read. It broke her heart.

"We understand if we have to go back," James said quietly, his voice barely above a whisper. Olivia nodded in agreement beside him, her eyes downcast.

Mya's heart twisted. She stepped forward, kneeling down in front of them, so they were eye level. "What do you mean? You two aren't going anywhere." She reached out, brushing a tear from Olivia's cheek. "You're staying with me."

James looked at her, his expression conflicted. "What if... what if we're just a burden?"

Mya shook her head firmly. "You are not a burden."

Olivia sniffled, wiping her nose with the back of her hand. "We just don't want to go back to the system."

Mya's heart broke for them. She gently cupped their faces in her hands, her voice filled with all the love she could offer. "You won't, you're with me now. Tomorrow, you'll have your first day of school." She smiled, trying to ease their worries. "Now, go inside, get showered, and get ready for bed. It's time for you both to get some rest."

Chapter 19

Carter

Carter walked through the front door, a heaviness weighing on his chest. Tracy was sprawled on the couch, her legs curled under her, scrolling through her phone like everything was normal. The house wasn't normal. It was messy, the kind of mess that made Carter pause. He'd never seen it like this before. There was a time when the apartment had felt cozy, neat, like a place to rest. Now, it just felt... empty.

Carter made his way to the kitchen, grabbed the milk from the fridge, and poured himself a glass. His fingers shook slightly as he spoke, voice rough. "You didn't think to clean up around here?"

Tracy barely looked up from her phone. "Well, hey, how you doin'? You could at least speak."

Carter didn't have the energy to fight. He walked towards the dining room table, eyes scanning the piles of dishes and clutter that made the apartment feel even more suffocating. Tracy finally sat up and moved toward him, her hand brushing against his arm as she sat down. He couldn't look at her.

She placed her hand on his, and for a moment. Carter felt like maybe things could work with Tracy. That thought quickly disappeared as his mind shifted to Mya how they had an actual life together and the only reason he was with Tracy was because she was available. He couldn't even hear Tracy's voice at first, just the sound of his own guilt echoing in his head.

"We really need a night out, babe," Tracy said softly, breaking the silence, but Carter wasn't listening.

His thoughts were a tangled mess. He pulled his hand back slowly, finally meeting Tracy's eyes. It wasn't Tracy he was looking at. It was Mya's face that haunted him, her disappointment, her tears. Suddenly, he couldn't hold it in any longer.

"Are you sure my son is my son?" he asked, his voice low but cutting through the air.

Tracy's expression changed instantly, her defensiveness creeping in. "What? Are you just gonna ignore everything I'm saying? I'm asking about going out like we used to, and you are going to ask me if he is your child? He looks like you don't he!"

The space between them growing wider. His voice was quiet, almost strained as he repeated, "Is my son my son? Not do he look like me."

Tracy shot up from her seat, her words sharp as she raised her voice. "Yes, of course, he's your son! What's with all the questions? Oh, you must have been hanging with wifey. I knew this was going to happen. I'm telling you now Carter I'm not the one to play with."

Carter's mind was racing, the knot in his stomach tightening. He rubbed his hands together, then pressed his face into his palms, as if the weight of it all would somehow disappear. "I don't get it Tracy" he muttered. "Me and Mya tried... We tried for so long. The doctor said it was on me, but here I am... I've got a kid with you. It just doesn't make sense."

The room felt colder. Tracy stood, her anger flaring as she shot back, "I don't know what's gotten into you, Carter. I'm not the type of woman to pin a baby on anyone. Don't get it twisted. You're staying at my place, and if it's that bad go back to her. Maybe she doesn't have what I have to produce a child!" With a flick of her hand, Tracy turned and walked into the bedroom slamming the door behind her. Carter stayed there, his body tense, every muscle stiff as he tried to breathe.

He leaned against the table, thoughts swirling. He thought he had it all figured out. That living with Tracy would give him some stability, some sense of control. Now, it felt like he was drowning. He could hear his own heartbeat in his ears

Hours later, Carter woke up to the faint sound of coffee brewing. The smell of it hit him before he even opened his eyes. Tracy was in the kitchen, still in her nightgown and bonnet, as though the world hadn't shifted in the last twenty-four hours.

Carter glanced at the kitchen, panic immediately setting in "What time is it?" he asked, voice hoarse from his restless sleep.

"It's 11 o'clock, I see you slept on the couch" Tracy answered without looking at him, sipping her coffee as she sat at the kitchen table.

Carter jumped up, grabbing his shoes in a hurry. "Crap, I forgot. I gotta go help my mama today." He didn't even stop to think as he rushed to the bathroom, brushing his teeth and throwing himself together.

As he walked out of the room, Tracy's eyes followed him, her voice laced with curiosity. "You in a rush, huh? You sure it's your mama and not wifey"

Carter didn't even pause. "Don't start Tracy, I'll see you later," he called over his shoulder, already halfway out the door. The faster he got out of here, the better.

Carter's truck screeched to a stop outside his mama's house. He was jumped out of the vehicle, nearly stumbling up the porch steps to where Mama Ruth was rocking in her chair, looking as steady as ever. She raised an eyebrow as he approached.

"Mama, I'm so sorry I overslept," Carter said quickly, trying to make up for his lack of attention.

Mama Ruth didn't immediately respond. Instead, she sighed deeply, her voice low and knowing. "Mmhm. You at that woman's house now oversleeping? That's sad, Carter. I had to hear in the streets that you're sleepin' with some woman in Spiral Hills... And Mya... that good ole girl shouldn't have to go through that. Then you had the nerve to be ignoring my phone calls."

Carter paused, guilt flooding his chest. "Mama, stop listening to everything you hear," he muttered, shifting uncomfortably as he picked up a few things from the porch.

Mama Ruth didn't miss a beat. "Mmhm. Don't lie to me now. When you done in the yard come in here and fix my TV. I want to be able to watch my good shows," she said, her tone gentle but firm.

Carter sighed but did as she asked. As he worked, his thoughts continued to swirl. He couldn't stop thinking about how he is about to have to explain this to his 65-year-old mother. She only thought the best about him, and now things are different. When he finished the repairs, he plopped down on the couch next to Mama Ruth, feeling some comfort of being home.

"What has gotten into you baby?" Mama Ruth asked, eyes narrowing as she studied him.

Carter looked down, his voice barely a whisper. "What you mean mama nothing has I'm okay, Mama."

Mama Ruth's eyes softened, but there was a glint of determination in them. "Carter Alexander Wright, I taught you better than this. Don't lie to me. Now what's really going on?"

Carter opened his mouth, but the words caught in his throat. He couldn't lie to her. Slowly, he let the truth spill out, his voice raw. "It wasn't like I planned to do this. Everybody keep asking like I planned to go out and do this. Stuff like this just happen. I didn't try to get caught up like this, but I did. And now... it can't be fixed."

Mama Ruth looked at him as though she had expected this. She wasn't angry, just steady. "Well, baby, what do you think happens when you go into a hornet's nest?" she said, her voice sharp. "This kind of thing don't happen. You let your mind and flesh get the best of you. You can't expect it to be easy. First you need to work on yourself. Go get you a job. Be a man, Carter. The man me and your father raised you to be. You let that one injury pull you completely out."

Carter looked at her, confusion still clouding his mind. "A job? I... I don't know what I'm supposed to do. Working a 9-5 was never my goal."

Mama Ruth's eyes softened again. "I always told Charles, that we were too soft on you. You're our first and only child, and he wanted you to live a good life. You need to get you some business about yourself, a job. Work on getting Mya back. You're not divorced yet. She's still your wife. She is not going to take you back to just start back taking care of you just because you didn't plan on having a 9-5. Find you something to do to become better."

Carter's breath caught in his throat. He had been trying to go back but Mya wasn't hearing that. By the looks of it Mya would never take him back. Hearing his mother say it made him wonder if it was possible if he showed Mya that he was working to be better.

Mama Ruth placed her hand on his arm. "I'm going to let you come live with me. You don't need to be living with that woman anymore. You know that kid ain't yours. You've got the same issues your daddy had."

Carter blinked, stunned. "What issues?"

Mama Ruth's voice softened. "That hard-to-have-kids issue. God will make a way for you and Mya just like God did for me and Charles. You're still married, so there's hope. You've got to fight. Become a better man. A woman loves a man who's got something going for himself. She doesn't need you to be rich, but she doesn't need you to be a burden either."

Carter felt the weight of her words sink in. He had been avoiding reality for too long. He was going to have to fight a different way not just begging and empty promises.

Mama Ruth gave him a nod, her face soft but firm. "Okay, go get your stuff. I'll be waiting on you. I don't know what you were doing there anyway."

As Carter made his way to the truck, he felt a strange sense of relief. He hated the idea of going back to his mama's house, hated the idea of having to start over in a place that reminded him of everything he had failed at. The truth was, it was better than nothing. Better than living in Tracy's mess.

He started the engine, his thoughts immediately turning to Mya. His chest tightened as he thought about her—her smile, her laugh, the way she cared for him even when he was broken.

Now... he was a fool, wrapped up in this mess with Tracy. He didn't even know how he'd ended up with her. He was doing well in high school, his knee injury had set him back, and that was when the depression crept in. Mya had stepped up, doing everything she could to take care of him, and he hadn't even realized how much she was carrying.

His hands gripped the steering wheel tighter as he pulled up to Jamal's house. He knocked on the door and waited, his mind still on Mya, but when the door opened, it wasn't his friend he saw first—it was Jamal's wife.

"Hey, Nancy," Carter said, forcing a small smile.

She looked him up and down, eyebrow raised. "Mmhm. Don't put that cheating spirit on my husband," she said, her tone sharp as she walked back to her room.

Carter shook his head, muttering to himself as he walked inside.

Jamal was sitting on the couch, already holding a controller. He glanced up and grinned. "What's good, broski?"

"My guy, my guy," Carter said, flopping down next to him.

Jamal handed him a controller. "Grab one. Let's run one."

They played for a few minutes, the tension between them palpable. Jamal didn't say anything at first, but Carter could feel his friend's curiosity. After a while, Jamal broke the silence. "So, man... what happening with you and Mya?"

Carter paused, the controller resting in his hand for a minute before he picked back up. "What you mean?"

Jamal shrugged, playing without looking up. "What y'all going to do?"

Carter hesitated, unsure how much he wanted to say. "Man, you know how it is. Mya just focused on herself now so she just working and ignoring me. She mad at me for messing up but what about what she did to lead me into this. Yeah, I messed up I got caught up in conversation, but Mya literally dropped me man, and you know it."

Jamal shot him a sideways glance, the game forgotten for a moment. "Man, nah. I don't get it. If it ain't Nancy, I'm not talking. How did you get mixed in with Tracy of all people."

Carter laughed dryly. "I hear you." He sighed, his mind slipping back to that night with Tracy. "Man, it was a rough night... Mya was in New York, living her dream and sending me pictures of herself having a good time, not even thinking about me. I was at the bar one night, and Tracy was there. It was like... like she didn't see the messed-up version of me. She saw the man I used to be, the one I wanted to be again. We talked for a bit, and she believed in me. I didn't have to worry about what I didn't have. She made me feel like a man again. It wasn't supposed to go far it was just supposed to be a conversation."

Jamal nodded slowly, sensing the shift in Carter's tone. "I get it, bro, but still... you could've talked to anybody. Now look at you, out here homeless."

Carter winced at the truth. "Tracy and I made plans, but I never thought about following through or for them to happen that fast. Tracy busted in that shop and ran her mouth. When I tried to end things with her a couple of years ago, she dropped the bomb. Told me she was pregnant. She said I had a kid on the way."

Jamal paused the game, his eyes wide. "Wait, bro... You have a kid? I'm an uncle? You turned a side chick into a main one."

Carter fiddled with his fingers, his stomach in a knot. "That's what she says."

Jamal's expression hardened. "Man, I'm your bro, but I know Mya's hurting right now. A whole baby bro."

Carter felt his chest tighten. He had known that he was breaking her heart. "I never wanted to hurt her. She was—she is the love of my life. I don't know how I let this... this mess get in the way."

Jamal sighed and set the controller down. "So, what you gonna do now?"

Carter looked at Jamal. "I'm gonna move back in with my mom. I will find a job and show Mya I'm man enough for her."

Jamal raised an eyebrow, a little skeptical. "Well, as long as you got a plan... I remember one time, I almost cheated on Nancy. I was crawling and crying back to her, but when I came at her as a man, she was ready to take me back. She didn't want no other woman getting all the work she'd put in."

Nancy's voice echoed from the other room. "Lie again, Jamal."

Both men burst out laughing, but Nancy appeared, hands on her hips, looking unimpressed. "You came in here crying, reading scriptures, and then you went to church, and haven't been back" she said, shaking her head. "Then I let you back."

Jamal smirked, looking at Carter. "See, when they're home 24/7, you don't get any privacy. Be glad she was in New York."

Carter laughed, finally feeling a little lighter. "I gotta get out of here. I need to pack up and leave Tracy's house."

Jamal nodded. "How you gonna break it to her?"

Carter exhaled deeply. "I don't know, man. I'm gonna get my wife back though. This right here not the move. All those kids in that tiny apartment."

From the back of the house, Nancy yelled out, "Period! Take yo butt back home."

Carter couldn't help but laugh.

Carter stepped out of Jamal's house; the engine hummed beneath him as he drove. The road feeling longer than it ever had before. He wasn't sure what to expect when he reached Tracy's place, but part of him just needed to end this chapter, whatever it was.

When Carter pulled up, he spotted Tina walking out of her apartment, her stride cool but deliberate. She glanced over and saw him, but her eyes quickly darted away, pretending like she didn't. Carter knew better. He knew she saw him.

He got out of the truck and walked toward her. Tina didn't even try to pretend anymore. As soon as he was close enough, she stopped, hands on her hips, eyes blazing with frustration. "What you want Carter?" she spat, her voice cutting through the air like a blade.

Carter looked down, "Tina, you know me. You know that's not my character."

Tina crossed her arms and let out a sharp laugh. "Yes, actually, I do know your character," she said, her tone dripping with sarcasm. "You treated her like crap all through high school, and she still stayed. Then you blow your knee out, and Mya steps in to take care of you. Then what do you do? You go out and get involved with some hood chic. I'm still trying to find the part where this isn't your character."

Carter clenched his jaw, looking away for a moment as if he could escape her words. He licked his lips, trying to hold it together. “I haven’t been the best, but I’m still her husband and it wasn’t all bad days. I don’t know why she wouldn’t tell y’all the good stuff too.”

Tina cut him off, her voice sharp. “Before you try to find a way to blame her for your lack of character, let me stop you right there. You’re not about to make her the reason you’re out here lost, confused, and making bad decisions. You need to own up to your own mess. She didn’t make you do anything. You chose this. You can holler all day long about how she wasn’t there, but that girl gave up a good life to come down here a build a better one with you. You chose Tracy out of all people.”

With a huff, she pushed past him, heading toward her old, beat-up car, her words still lingering in the air like an echo. Carter stood there, feeling like the ground had shifted beneath him. He’d always prided himself on being understood, but in this moment, it felt like no one saw his side of the story—not even Tina. Everyone only saw her. They all saw Mya, the strong one, the one who had it all together. However, no one saw him. No one saw how much he'd been carrying how he had taken care of his parents, how his dad had passed, how his dreams had shattered with that knee injury. He’d been broken, and Mya was the one who stayed. When she left, she walked away from everything he needed, not thinking about him, not realizing that he’d needed her in ways he couldn’t articulate. When she came back, it was as if everything was on her terms, when she was ready.

The apartment was eerily quiet when Carter walked in. It was spotless—cleaner than he before. Tracy waited till he left and cleaned up.

He stood there for a second, his hand resting on the doorframe of the bedroom. When his eyes landed on Tracy, lying there on the bed, fast asleep, something in him recoiled.

This wasn't the place he needed to be anymore. This wasn't the life he wanted.

His gaze lingered on her for a moment, his heart torn. This was the moment he could silently slip away, make a break for it. As he stood there, he realized that leaving without saying anything would only add to the pile of lies and half-truths he'd already told. He owed her some kind of explanation. Even if it didn't fix everything, he had love for her.

He walked to the small table by the window and grabbed the pen and back of the kids coloring sheet. The words came out slowly, each one feeling heavier than the last.

"I'm so sorry for this. I need to step away to get my head from being clouded. I'm so sorry Trace."

It wasn't much, but it was all he could manage at the moment. He didn't want to give her any false hope. He folded the paper and left it on the counter, then grabbed his bags. He took one last look around the apartment. At the place that had, for a time felt like his escape, but now only felt like a prison.

Carter slammed the truck door behind him and started the engine, the road ahead was clear. His thoughts were already back with Mya. He didn't know what would happen when he saw her, but he had to try. He couldn't keep living like this.

He headed straight for her house.

Carter's truck rolled to a stop in front of the house he and Mya once called home. The place looked different, but in a way, it still felt familiar—like the echo of old memories clung to the walls. He knocked on the door with a little uncertainty, hoping to find some kind of clarity or closure. James opened it, squinting when he saw who it was.

"She isn't here," James said, his voice flat.

Carter nodded, taking in the silence that hung in the air. "Okay," he said, turning to leave, then adding, "uh you're looking strong, James."

James stared at him for a moment, clearly puzzled. He didn't remember Carter right away. Carter chuckled, shaking his head. "Well, shut the door and lock it, man. Don't just open the door for anybody." James watched him walk away, still trying to place him.

Carter made his way back to his truck. He grabbed his phone and quickly texted Mya.

"Hey, just wanted to let you know I stopped by the house. I left Tracy's house. I'm done with her and would really like to talk with you."

He hit send, then started the engine, feeling a little lighter, but still unsure. Was she even ready to talk to me? he wondered. He pulled out of the driveway, heading back to his mama's house.

As he drove, his eyes caught sight of Pastor walking into the church.

He pulled into the church parking lot and got out, catching Pastor's attention right away. Pastor's face lit up when he saw him. "Carter! Boy, what are you doing here!" Pastor called out, his voice warm, and full of joy.

Carter chuckled, "What's good, Pastor? How you been?"

Pastor paused, studying Carter for a moment. "Your spirit lookin' clearer, son. Look like a free man."

Carter laughed softly, surprised by the observation. "I feel clear, Pastor."

The pastor's face softened. "Well, what's on your mind?

You need something?"

Carter hesitated before speaking, something in him wanting to let out all the chaos he was feeling. "I saw you walkin' in the church and thought I should stop by. I wanted to let you know I left that woman and packed my things. I don't have Mya back, but I'm headed to my mom's place."

Pastor's eyes lit up with genuine joy. "Praise God! That's good, son. I'm glad you finally decided to fight for what matters. There ain't nothin' better than being a man and getting your priorities together."

Carter nodded, though he wasn't sure what that really meant just yet. "Yeah, I'm gonna go find me a job and get things together."

Pastor looked at him, thoughtful. "That's a start. Well, what do you like to do, Carter? What's your passion?"

Carter looked down for a moment, reflecting. "I like sports, but I'm putting that in the past. I'm pretty good at painting and building, working with my hands and stuff. My dad taught me before he died."

Pastor's face broke into a smile. "Well, let me be the first to hire you. We got some painting and building projects we need help with around here. I'm pretty sure some of my members do to."

Carter blinked in surprise. "For real? I wasn't expecting that."

Pastor laughed. "God says He'll bless the works of your hands, son. I want to see you do good in life, and I know God wants that too. The next step is getting involved with a community of men and learning who God has called you to be. We have men's Bible Study tonight. I want you to come."

Carter hesitated, his nerves getting the best of him. "Pastor, I don't even have a suit, or a Bible..."

Pastor reached over to a table, grabbed his Bible, and handed it to Carter. "You can have mine. You don't need to dress up. We're men. We're not here to look pretty, just to get right with God."

Carter stood there for a moment, his hand on the Bible, overwhelmed by the simple kindness of it. This wasn't what he expected, but somehow it was exactly what he needed. He took the Bible, nodding as if he was finally finding some solid ground.

"Pastor, I... I don't know what to say. I appreciate this, seriously."

"I want to see you here tonight," Pastor said with a smile. "Just come as you are. No dress up close needed."

As Carter walked back to his truck, holding the Bible in his hands, a tear slipped down his cheek. He wasn't sure why he was crying, but the weight of it all—the love, the care, the forgiveness hit him in a way he didn't expect. This is what I've been missing, he thought. This is what I've been looking for.

When he got back to his mama's house, she was resting in her room, Carter felt a sense of peace just being back in this space. It wasn't glamorous, but it was familiar. He walked into his old high school room—still the same. The basketball posters, the picture of him and Mya on prom night and just when they were hanging out, the old bean bag, the desk where he spent hours dreaming. It all felt like a lifetime ago, but here he was, back to the beginning.

He threw his bag on the bed and stood there for a moment, staring at the room. "Sometimes you gotta go back to the root to overcome the past," he muttered to himself, though it didn't fully sink in just yet.

Then his phone buzzed. A text from Mya. He opened it.

"Okay, that's good for you. Next time let me know before you just pop up at the house."

The words stung, cold and distant. Is that it? he thought.

The doubts swirled in his mind, but then he remembered his mama's words, "You aren't divorced yet. God has a plan for your marriage."

Chapter 20
Tracy

Tracy rubbed her eyes and rolled over in bed, slowly waking to the silence in the house. Slipping out of bed, she padded into the kitchen wearing nothing but her bonnet and a nightgown that stopped just above her knees. The night light streamed in through the window as she yawned, stretched, and made her way to the kitchen. She poured her some tea, took a deep breath, then leaned against the counter while checking her phone.

A sudden knock on the door interrupted the stillness.

Bang. Bang. Bang.

Tracy groaned, sipped her tea, and shuffled over to the front door. She cracked it open.

"What do you want?" she asked flatly.

Ray Ray stood there, face tense. "Here, shawty."

He handed her a folded piece of paper. She snatched it out of his hand.

"What is this?" Tracy said looking confused.

Ray Ray didn't flinch. "Read it. That child ain't mine. You lied to me. You gon' get enough of doing what you doing."

Tracy's heart skipped. Her throat felt dry. "There must be a big mistake, she is your daughter" she said, coughing.

"Nope," Ray said, shaking his head, "no mistake. How you going to tell a test that it's a mistake. C'mon Tracy We did a full DNA test—twice. She's not mine, so stop playin' in my face and causing mess."

He turned and started walking off, then paused, turned back around, and snatched the paper from her hand.

"I'll send you a picture of it," he muttered. "Now stop tellin' folks that's my kid. I feel sorry for the little girl... cause I actually love her. You had me and Tina taking care of her, but she ain't mine. Go find her real father."

Without another word, he walked to his beat-up car, got in, and pulled off, leaving Tracy standing there in the doorway numb.

She slammed the door shut, her breath shaky. She rushed to her bedroom, throwing on some clothes and brushing her teeth in a hurry. Her mind was racing, heart pounding.

As she stepped into the hallway, her eyes landed on something sitting on the table.

A note.

She reached for it, hands trembling, and unfolded the paper.

It was from Carter.

He was gone.

Her mouth dropped open. The keys in her hand slipped to the floor with a loud clang. A single tear rolled down her cheek as she stared at the words of his pitiful goodbye letter—empty, final, and devastating.

She was alone.

Tracy stared at the door, still holding the note in her hand. Her face twisted with disbelief.

"I know he did not just do this," she muttered. "After I interrupted my whole life for his? Just for him to run back to his little wife?"

She scoffed, tossing the paper aside. "He must think he slick. Think I'm just gonna let him go? He got another thing coming."

Tracy paced the kitchen, fuming.

"I'm in here cookin', cleanin', raising his child, and now he wanna go play family with her? Ha! Nahhh. Everything he got with that wife of his, that's just as much mine, and my son's."

She wiped her face quickly, snatched up her purse, and grabbed her phone. She dialed a lawyer as she stormed out of the house, keys jingling in her hand. Her mind was already made up she wasn't letting this go. Not while she was the one raising all these kids, carrying the weight of the life he said they'd have.

Tracy drove straight to Pam's house. She needed to vent, needed someone who'd hype her up, not calm her down.

As she pulled up, a couple of big, buff dudes were walking out. Tracy stepped out of her car just as Pam opened the door, looking around with suspicion.

When she spotted Tracy, Pam's face lit up.

"TRACYYYY! GIRL, COME ON UP HERE!"

Tracy laughed, stepping onto Pam's raggedy porch. That porch had been falling apart since they were kids. Pam's house had always been a kind of juke joint. Her mama ran a little store inside it, and Pam had kept the hustle going. The roof looked like it was about to cave in, but it was still her home.

Inside, the heat hit hard. Pam turned to her, fanning herself.

"You want something to drink? Girl, I just got my stamps, so kitchen is full!"

Tracy nodded. "Yeah, let me get a fruit punch."

Pam grabbed it from the fridge and plopped down on the couch beside her. "So... what did I do to get this visit?"

Tracy rolled her eyes and sipped her drink. "So, you know me and Carter had a little thing going on, right?"

Pam raised an eyebrow. "Mmhmm…"

"Well, how 'bout he thinks he just gon' up and leave now that his little wife back in town. He tryna get it right with her I guess after he been living with me for the past two years!"

Pam leaned in, legs open like a dude, propping her elbow on her knee. “I know you lying! What he think this is?”

“That’s what I said!” Tracy threw her hands up. “He gon’ have to give me everything he promised. Then I had his son, and he think he can just up and leave.”

“He sure is,” Pam said, nodding. “You got all the proof. I would file a report. Handle him and that little wife, too. If he going to be with her then they both need to be taking care of that child.”

“Oh, don’t worry. I am,” Tracy said, her voice low and serious.

Pam wiped her face dramatically, her eyelashes so long she could barely see. “Girl, I can’t believe his wife still want him after all he been doing.”

“She must be desperate,” Tracy muttered.

Pam stood up and flipped on the ceiling fan. The house barely had air, and the heat was unbearable.

“My Aunt Rudene know a real good lawyer,” Pam said. “That’s how she got her baby daddy. Girl, she took everything. Little Darnell living real good now. I’m telling you her lawyer is who you need!”

Tracy grinned. “I need that number.”

“I’m gon’ call her,” Pam said, grabbing her phone. “Tracy, you need to take everything. Don’t let him just get away with this. He’s playin’ with your heart, actin’ like y’all were gon’ be a family, just to run back to her while you stuck with his kid.

The kid he made with you while he was married."

Tracy took a breath. "That's not even the worst part."

Pam looked over, curious. "What you mean?"

"How about Shaunie is not Ray Ray's child."

Pam's eyes nearly bulged out of her head. "GIRLLLL, WHAT?!"

Tracy shook her head, staring down at the floor. "He went and got a DNA test. Brought the results over this morning. She's not his."

Pam threw her hands up. "What in the world? Since when do hood dudes start learning about DNA tests!"

Tracy pressed her lips together. "When did Ray Ray even have the time? I bet it was Tina. Shaunie always with her."

"Girl, I doubt Tina helped with that. She just another hood rat," Pam said, brushing it off.

"Well, you know they all friends—her and Carter's wife, best friends. That whole little circle wants to be so much."

Pam rolled her eyes. "So, you just wrapped up in mess with all these wanna-be-rich chics."

Tracy let out a tired sigh. "Looks like it, and he acted like he wasn't involved with them as if he had nothing to do with any of them."

Pam was still fanning herself with that bent-up envelope, sweat shining on her forehead.

"Ain't no way, Carter played you until his wife got back. If I were you, I would make sure he paid for it all!" she muttered, shaking her head as she plopped back down on the couch.

She looked over at Tracy with narrowed eyes. "You need to do whatever you can to make sure you and your kids are straight. Carter's wife is loaded, and if she's back with him, then guess what? His son is her responsibility now too."

Tracy nodded slowly. "Sure is. but I want Carter. He was such a good man. I'm so mad I fell for him the way I did."

Pam pressed her lips together and gave her a look. "Good man? What about him is good? He was cheating on his wife with you. Right now, is not the time to be looking for love from him. Right now, you need to take care of yourself."

Tracy's eyes dropped to the floor. "I know," she said softly. "But he was a lot of help. He cleaned good, helped with the kids, and… his touch was so smooth and just right."

Pam rolled her eyes. "Girl, you can find any man with a good touch. That ain't special. You can't make a man stay just 'cause you want him to. He gonna make his own decision anyway. So, you need to do what's best for you."

Tracy took another slow sip of her fruit punch, her thoughts swirling. The front door opened and someone walked in, talking loudly and laughing. The sound of work boots hitting the floor filled the space.

Pam stood up, adjusting her top. "Well, girl, my customers just got off the warehouse shift. I gotta make this money. We'll talk later."

Tracy stood too, clutching her bag close. She nodded and headed toward the door.

Chapter 21

Mya J

Mya was in the back of her store, sorting through some merchandise. The store wasn't as busy as it had been lately, and she had the space to think. As she moved around, her mind wandered, imagining what she wanted for the future of the shop.

Her phone buzzed in her pocket. Carter's name popped up on the screen. She stared at it for a second, considering whether she should even bother looking at the message. "Me and Tracy done. Can we talk." She almost laughed out loud.

Oh, so now you want to talk, huh? Mya thought, feeling that familiar bitterness creep in. "I was steak when you were sneaking with mashed potatoes, but now those pockets empty and you want to come back."

She shook her head and ignored the message. She wasn't about to run back to him just because he'd decided to jump ship. He made his bed, now he could lie in it. She needed a distraction, so she decided to call up Diana and Tina.

The phone rang once before Diana picked up, "Hey girl?"

Tina's voice followed, "what's going on?"

Mya smirked, ready to spill the tea. "Guess what, y'all."

Both paused for a moment. "What?" they asked in unison.

Mya grinned, holding up her phone to her ear. "How about I get a text from Carter saying he left Tracy."

There was a long pause before they responded in unison. "Whhaaat?" Diana exclaimed.

Tina's voice was laced with disbelief. "Mhm. I saw him coming in as I was leaving, I knew it looked like he was up to something."

Mya raised an eyebrow. "Hold up, they stays by you?"

Diana's voice was low and knowing. "Uh-oh, here it comes."

Tina paused for a second before responding, "Girl me and Diana found out they did the other day. I saw him going in, and we were walking towards each other, and I let him have it."

Mya laughed. "So, he was over there by you the whole time?"

Tina was speechless. All she could say was "Girl I promise I didn't find out till the other day."

Diana's voice softened, "So, Mya, how did that text make you feel?"

Mya sighed, leaning against the counter. "Honestly, I don't feel any way. I've kind of settled myself. I'm over it." She shrugged, trying to make it sound like she wasn't hurt, even though a little part of her was.

Tina leaned back in her chair at home, a knowing smile playing on her lips. "Mhm, there must be someone else," she said, her tone teasing.

Mya, on the other end of the line, chuckled. "Speaking of someone else, how about Chase called me."

Tina fell silent, shocked into quiet thinking that Mya someone else was Chase.

Diana, who had been part of their three-way call, raised an eyebrow. "Is that who you are talking to now Mya?"

Mya smiled, even though they couldn't see her. "Girl no, but Tina is."

Tina quickly coughed finding her voice. "Oh hush, it was one date."

"It wasn't just one date. He said y'all are getting to know each other very well." Mya said, amused.

"He reached out to me," Tina admitted, unable to hide a small smile.

"He said he had a real good time," Mya confessed.

Diana gasped dramatically. "Oh Lord, I know you didn't give it up to him Tina."

Tina laughed. "No, I didn't. I know how to keep my pearls in my pocketbook."

Diana and Mya burst out laughing.

Just then, a customer walked into Mya's store. "Y'all come over tonight," Mya said quickly. "Someone just walked in the store."

They ended the call, and Mya turned her attention to the customer. "How can I help you?" she asked, putting on her professional demeanor.

The woman standing before her held out an envelope. "Are you Mya Jean Wright?" she asked.

"Yes, I am," Mya replied, a sense of unease creeping in.

The woman handed her the envelope. "You have been served," she said curtly before turning and walking out.

Mya stood there, stunned. What else could go wrong? she thought. When I was in New York, none of this was happening.

She stared at the envelope, dreading what it might contain. "I know he didn't just serve me divorce papers," she muttered to herself.

Her hands trembled as she opened the envelope, her heart pounding in her chest. As she read the contents, her eyes widened in disbelief. She was being sued by Tracy!

"I know this chick didn't!" Mya exclaimed, her anger flaring.

Without wasting a moment, she took pictures of the documents and sent them to her group chat with Diana and Tina, her mind racing with thoughts of what to do next.

Mya stared at her phone, still processing what she had just read in the legal papers. Her hands shook as she typed out a message to Diana and Tina.

Mya: "Y'all not gonna believe this. Tracy is suing me."

Within seconds, her phone buzzed with a quick reply.

Diana: "OMG, girl, are you serious?"

Tina: "What in the world???"

Mya sighed, unable to hold back the frustration. She glanced at the papers again, the words still sinking in. She quickly typed back.

Mya: "Yes. I'm shocked too."

Diana and Tina didn't waste time texting each other privately.

Diana: "Let's go to the shop. To check on her."

A short while later, Diana and Tina pulled up to the store. Mya was standing behind the counter, trying to pull herself together. When she saw them walk through the door, she was relieved, but also nervous.

The store was eerily quiet, nothing like the usual hustle and bustle she was used to. Her eyes scanned the room, and she couldn't help but feel a pang of unease.

Tina was the first to break the silence. "Where's London?"

Mya leaned on the counter, her voice a little flat. "I gave her some time off. She's been handling everything here on her own since we've been here, and she needed this break." "Isn't that her job?" Tina said.

Diana, her expression a mix of concern and determination, walked straight up to Mya. "Let me see the papers."

Mya handed them over without a word, watching as Diana quickly scanned them. Diana's frown deepened with each line she read, and when she was done, she shook her head.

"This girl has no case, Mya. You need to stop stressing about it. Did you tell Carter?"

Mya ran her fingers through her hair, pacing in the small space behind the counter. "No. I can't believe he got us mixed up in this. I've never been this type of girl. I just... I just want to move forward. Why would he get involved in some mess like this? I have nothing to do with Tracy."

Tina folded her arms, her voice soft but firm. "Don't put this on you. You need to tell him what's going on. He's the one who's dragging you into it. What is she suing you for, anyway?"

Diana glanced down at the papers again. "She's suing you for threatening her and defaming her character." Diana's voice hardened as she read on. "When I'm done with her, she won't have a case. Trust me."

Mya not worried about anything Diana is saying all she could focus on was the right now. Diana was always the calm in the storm. Then Diana's face shifted, and she looked back up at Mya. "And... Carter promised her that this store would be hers. That's what she's claiming. She thinks she's entitled to it because of some promise he made. Also, her son is as well."

Mya's heart sank. "Wait, what? This girl is trying to take my store.Carter doesn't even have the means to promise her anything! He never bought this place. This store is mine—my hard work, my vision..."

Before Mya could finish, the bell above the door jingled, signaling someone's arrival. Mya looked up, but her heart dropped when she saw a police officer standing in the doorway. His expression was neutral, but his presence immediately brought a wave of dread.

The officer took a step inside, and Mya instinctively moved away from the counter, trying to keep her composure. "How can I help you?"

He looked directly at her. "Are you Mya Jean Wright?"

Her stomach twisted. "Yes, I am."

The officer sighed, pulling out some official looking documents. "I'm sorry to inform you, but we are closing your store down due to its involvement in an ongoing investigation." Mya's world tilted. She stared at the officer for a moment; tears begin to form, then looked to Diana and Tina, her heart racing as panic gripped her chest. The words barely left her mouth.

Diana stepped forward, her protective instincts kicking in. "What case? What investigation?"

The officer handed the documents to Diana, his eyes flicking between the three of them. "This case involves the claims from Tracy. She's the one behind the allegations."

Mya felt her legs wobble, her emotions spiraling out of control. She could feel the tears falling, she fell to the floor having the wind knock her off her feet.

Tina was visibly furious, her fists clenched. "It's that heffa! She's the one behind all this mess! I'm about to handle her. I swear I am."

Mya screamed, her voice raw with tears and with frustration. "No, Tina, don't." The tears started to fall, streaming down her cheeks.

Tina froze. Diana shot her a look, then turned to Mya. The concern in her eyes was clear. However, Mya wasn't done yet.

She wiped her face with the back of her hand and stood up. "I need to grab my purse. I can't... I can't take this anymore."

Diana nodded, stepping aside as Mya moved to the counter, grabbed her purse, and wiped her face. The papers the officer had handed her still sat on the counter, and she snatched them up, clutching them tightly in her hand.

She looked at Diana. "You got this?"

Diana gave her a firm nod. "I sure do."

With that, Mya took a steadying breath, wiping her tears away. She turned to Tina, who still looked ready to throw down. "Come on y'all."

Diana gave a sharp nod, and together, they walked out of the shop, leaving the officer standing there. As they reached the door, Mya's heart sank even further when she saw the officer walking outside, unfurling store closed tape that stretched across the storefront.

Her brand-new store—the dream she'd worked so hard for was now sealed off. The reality of it all hit her like a ton of bricks. She wasn't just being attacked by Tracy; now, her whole life was being turned upside down, and she wasn't sure how much more she could take.

Diana, sitting beside her, reached over and gently placed a hand on her shoulder. Tina was on the other side, her arm around Mya's back, offering comfort in silence. They shared her pain in that moment, their solidarity more valuable than any words could be.

"Thanks, y'all," Mya whispered, her voice thick with emotion. She didn't have the strength to say much else. She didn't need to. Diana squeezed her shoulder reassuringly, and Tina shot her a look that promised things weren't over.

"We're here, Mya. We got you," Diana said quietly.

With one last look at her store—the place she'd poured everything into what was supposed to save her marriage; Mya finally nodded. "I'm going to head home."

When Mya pulled into her driveway, she felt like a weight had settled in her chest. She wasn't sure if she was relieved to be away from the situation or just numb from everything that had happened. As she stepped inside the house, something completely unexpected caught her off guard.

The entire house was spotless.

The kids had gone above and beyond, everything in perfect order. The living room, kitchen, and even the kids' rooms were neatly arranged. Mya stood in the doorway for a moment, completely stunned. She hadn't asked them to do this, but somehow, they had taken the initiative. It was the last thing she expected after the kind of day she'd had.

Olivia appeared from the hallway, her eyes lighting up when she saw Mya. "Hey."

James appeared in the doorway just then, walking over to her and sitting down beside her. The moment he sat down, he looked at her with a quiet sincerity.

"Thank you," James said, his voice soft but heavy with meaning. "Thank you for everything, for all you've done for us."

Mya blinked, the floodgates threatening to open again. She wasn't sure if it was the exhaustion or the overwhelming weight of the day, but those simple words from her James meant more than anything. He hadn't said much, but those words had been enough to fill a space inside her that had felt empty for so long.

Chapter 22

Carter

Carter pulled into the parking lot of the church, scanning the rows for an empty spot. The lot wasn't as crowded as he expected, which gave him a sense of relief. Less people, less attention, he thought to himself, grateful for the quiet. He wasn't sure what exactly he was expecting tonight, but the calm vibe suited him just fine.

He sat there for a moment, looking around at the other cars. He wasn't sure why, but he felt like tonight was a chance for him to reset, to reflect.

After a few minutes, he decided it was time to head inside. As he walked toward the entrance, he could already hear the murmur of men chatting and laughing. It wasn't as rowdy as he imagined, more like a group of men genuinely coming together.

Carter pushed the door open and entered the sanctuary. Immediately, Pastor Johnson's eyes found him from across the room. With a bright smile, the pastor made his way over, extending a hand.

"Carter! You made it. Praise God!" Pastor Johnson greeted him with warmth, his voice filled with excitement.

Carter shook the pastor's hand and responded, "Yes, sir I gave you my word," giving him a respectful nod.

Pastor Johnson, dressed in his usual button-down shirt and khakis with a sweater draped over his shoulders, looked at him approvingly. "Well, grab you some coffee and refreshments.

Make yourself at home," he said, waving toward a small table set up near the back of the room.

Carter nodded and walked over to the table, picking up a cup of coffee. He glanced around at the other men—most were dressed casually, but neat some in polo shirts, others in jackets. He stood out in his white t-shirt, jeans, and worn-out pair of Air Force Ones, but it didn't bother him. He wasn't here to impress anyone.

Taking a sip of his coffee, Carter found a seat toward the back, settling in the last row of the sanctuary. He didn't mind being on the outskirts. Being alone didn't bother him. The less attention, the better.

As the chatter from the men slowly died down, Pastor Johnson walked to the front and grabbed the microphone. His voice echoed through the speakers, commanding attention.

"Praise the Lord, everybody!" Pastor called out with energy, his voice filling the space. "We're about to get started. If everyone could please take your seats."

People shuffled into their chairs, and Carter watched as a few men moved in closer to him. He felt their presence and glanced up, wondering if Pastor had told them to sit near him. Some of the men had already paired up, chatting with old friends, while others hesitantly took the seats next to him. He figured it was probably just a way to welcome him new guy in the group. However still, Carter couldn't shake the feeling of being somewhat out of place.

Pastor Johnson stood at the front, his tone shifting from casual to reverent. "I'm so glad to have you all here tonight. We're going to dive right into the Word," he said, looking out over the room. "First, I want to remind you all that God has you right where He wants you. Whatever is happening in your life right now, whatever struggles or challenges you're facing, know that God is using those situations to shape and cultivate you into the men of God you are called to be."

Carter sat there, feeling the words hit him harder than he expected. It was like Pastor Johnson was speaking directly to him, as if God was sending him a message through this sermon.

The pastor spoke about trials, growth, and transformation, reminding them all that no matter how difficult things might seem, they were all on a path toward something greater. The message wasn't just about religion, it was about life, about strength, about resilience. Carter had always thought of church as a place for people to go and sit, to hear about God and then go back to their normal lives. However tonight, it felt different.

When the service finally ended, Carter stayed around and mingled with some of the guys, but his mind kept drifting back to the sermon. He overheard a conversation happening near the refreshments table.

One of the guys, a tall guy with a beard, was talking to another man in low tone, but the mention of a certain boutique caught Carter's attention.

"Did you hear about that new boutique that opened on 42nd St? It's already shut down," the guy said, shaking his head. "It's like they can't have anything nice without something going wrong."

Carter froze, his heart skipping a beat. His first thought was of Mya the boutique, the location... it all added up.

He couldn't help himself. He walked over to the group. "Wait, what shop?" he asked, trying to sound casual, though a twinge of anxiety crept into his voice.

"The one on 42nd St," the guy replied, looking at him like he should already know. "That new women's store. It was doing well, but now... no one knows what happened."

Carter's stomach dropped. He knew exactly what shop they were talking about. Panic surged through him, and without another word, he turned to Pastor Johnson.

"Pastor, I'm sorry, but I've got to head out," Carter said quickly, already walking toward the exit.

Pastor Johnson looking thankful that Carter even came "Alright, Carter. Glad you came."

Carter rushed out of the church, barely aware of the cold air that greeted him as he stepped outside. He jumped into his car and sped off, the only thought on his mind, Mya.

Carter pulled up outside Mya's house, his heart pounding as he parked his truck. He took a deep breath, reminding himself that he needed to check on her, but not try to force himself back in her heart.

He stepped out of the truck and walked to the front door, hoping she would hear him out. As he pressed the doorbell, his eyes caught the familiar sight of her walking toward the door. Carter quickly walked away from the door.

When Mya came outside, she walked toward him with that same confidence she always had. Tonight, she was more than just confident, she looked effortlessly beautiful. Her natural hair was pulled up into a messy high bun, and she wore a fitted t-shirt that hugged her curves perfectly, paired with leggings that showed off her long, toned legs. She looked as though she hadn't even tried, and yet, in that moment, she was glowing more than ever.

Carter couldn't help but look. It was the way she carried herself, the way her brown eyes met his, the way she seemed to be both familiar and untouchable all at once. He had always been drawn to her, but tonight seeing her like this he realized just how deep his feelings ran. He wasn't sure how he ended up here, but in this moment, everything felt so real, so raw.

Mya stopped in front of him, looking up at him with those big brown eyes, her gaze unwavering. "What is it, Carter?" she asked, her voice calm but carrying a subtle edge.

Carter hesitated for a moment, trying to steady himself. "I heard about the store. What happened?" His words felt heavier than he intended.

Mya's eyes widened slightly, and she exhaled in disbelief. "You've got to be kidding me," she muttered, her voice thick with frustration. She took a small step back, her arms crossed in front of her. She paused; disbelief still written all over her face. "Carter, Tracy is suing me. She's saying I defamed her character. She's claiming that the store is what you promised her like its half hers. Thinking because she has a kid with you that they have rights to my stuff!"

Carter felt his stomach drop. He couldn't believe what he was hearing. Tracy... Of course she would do something like this, he thought to himself. However, hearing Mya say it out loud made it hit harder.

"She thinks half of it is yours Carter," Mya continued, her eyes sharp. "You know... because you promised her this. Another one of your empty promises destroying my life." Carter's mind spun, trying to process the information. "We aren't even divorced," he said, his voice low, almost pleading for her to understand. "This shouldn't be happening.
How is that even possible, I left her."

Mya looked away for a moment, her face hardening as she sighed deeply. "Yeah, I know, but you went and created a new family who thinks they are entitled to my stuff." she said, barely above a whisper. Her gaze softened briefly but then hardened again as she met his eyes. "You brought this mess into my life. I never asked for any of this. Every time I try to move on your mess keeps popping back up."

Carter's heart squeezed painfully in his chest. He couldn't argue with her. She was right. This was all his fault. "Mya, this is all my fault," he said, his voice cracking with regret. "Baby, I'm trying. I'll fix this. I swear I will. I will talk with Tracy."

Mya shot him a look that stopped him in his tracks. "Fix this?" She scoffed, shaking her head in disbelief. "Carter, you brought that woman into our lives, into my life. Now you want to fix it. How do you even begin to fix something like this when it never had to happen?"

Carter looked at her, feeling the weight of her words pressing down on him. He knew she was angry, but there was no denying it she was right. He had destroyed everything they had built, and now, the consequences were spiraling out of control.

"I know I made my mistake," he said softly, his voice almost a whisper.

Mya let out a bitter laugh. "Mistake?" she repeated, her voice cutting through the night air. "This isn't some little error, Carter. This is big. This is real life. Now, you want to fix it. You shouldn't have created this false reality." Her words hit him like a slap in the face, and he couldn't even argue with her.

Carter was speechless. All he could do was stand there, drowning in the reality of what he had done. He had hurt her in ways that he wasn't sure he could ever fix.

"What do you want me to do, then?" he finally asked, desperation creeping into his voice. "Tell me what you want me to do. I'll do anything, just—"

Mya cut him off with a shrug of her shoulders. "Nothing," she said quietly. "Diana's got it." She met his gaze once more, and in that brief, piercing moment, Carter saw everything that had been broken between them, and it hurt.

"I gotta go," she said then, turning away. "It's getting late better get to whoever house you're staying at."

Carter watched her as she walked back toward the door. The sound of her footsteps was the only thing filling the heavy silence between them. When she reached the door, she didn't look back—just opened it, walked inside, and closed it behind her.

He stood there, frozen for a moment, staring at the door. A moment later, the porch light clicked off, and Carter's heart sank deeper into his chest. It was as if the light going out symbolized the last bit of hope he had left.

Leaning back against his truck, Carter exhaled deeply, his eyes cast toward the sky. "Jesus," he muttered, as if asking for help or maybe just for some kind of sign that everything wasn't completely lost.

With a heavy heart, he got back in his truck. He had nowhere else to go—not right now. His mind was a mess, his emotions a whirlwind. He needed to talk to someone who might understand. He couldn't face Mya anymore tonight not after that argument.

He put the truck in gear, and as he drove toward his mother's house, he wondered if there was any way to undo the damage he had caused. Would Mya ever forgive him? Or had he lost her for good?

Carter walked through the front door of his mother's house, the weight of the day hanging heavy on his shoulders. The house was quiet, the lights dimmed, and he could see from the hallway that his mama was already asleep.

He made his way to his old room flopped down on the bed, not bothering to change out of his clothes. He grabbed the bible Pastor gave to him earlier. He stared at it for a moment, unsure of what to do.

Without thinking, he opened it, as his eyes landed on the first page, a note written in Pastor handwriting caught his attention.

"Whoever I give this Bible to; I ask that you take a minute to pause and know that God loves you and created you for such a time as this. In this Bible, you will see my notes. Use them as a guide into learning and journeying with God."

Carter's eyes welled with tears as he read the pastor's words. How did Pastor know? He thought. As much as Carter tried to fight it, the tears began to fall.

With trembling hands, Carter sat up and began to look through the Bible, allowing the words to wash over him.

He closed the Bible gently and set it aside, his heart heavy but his spirit yearning. He needed God. He needed God more than anything, more than his regrets, more than his mistakes. Carter wasn't sure where to start, or if God would even listen. He had made such a mess of everything.

The silence in the room was deafening, and for the first time in a long while, Carter let his guard down. He bowed his head, his heart swelling with emotion, and he whispered a prayer.

"God… it's like things get worse, but somehow, it feels like You're getting closer to me. I don't know how or why, but I feel you with me right now. I need You, Lord. My marriage is falling apart, and I'm the one who wrecked it. I ruined it, God, but… I need You to fix it. I need You to fix me. I don't know how to do this on my own anymore. I can't fix this, but You can. I need You, Lord. I need Your guidance." His voice trembled as he continued.

"Lord, I know I've made mistakes, but I'm asking You to help me become not just a better man, but a man of God. I will become the man You created me to be. I will do better. I will live better. God, I surrender my life to You. Take it all. Take my mess, my heart, my mistakes… I give it all over to You."

Carter's body shook with the weight of the words. His knees hit the floor as he fell to the ground, his face pressed against the carpet as he cried, his tears mixing with the prayers.

Not my will, but Your will.

Chapter 23
Diana

Diana walked into her dining room, where Ray Ray was already sitting, dressed casually in a white t-shirt, black jeans, and a hat that hinted at a lack of recent haircuts. He had that easy confidence about him, the kind that came naturally to those dark-skinned men with light brown eyes and perfect white teeth—he didn't have to try too hard, and yet, it was clear why Tina kept going back to him.

She paused for a moment, taking in the sight of him, before shaking it off.

"I'm sorry about the wait," Diana said, finally stepping into the room.

Ray Ray, leaning back in his chair with that laid-back hood attitude, flashed a cool smile. "Nah, nah, you good."

Diana sat down across from him, her expression serious. "First thing I need to ask you did you, do it?"

Ray Ray didn't hesitate. His dark eyes met hers, unwavering. "No, I didn't do it."

Diana glanced down at the paperwork in front of her, the evidence she'd gathered. "Well, they're saying they've got witnesses who saw you break into cars and then run out of the parking lot."

Ray Ray leaned forward slightly, his voice steady. "See, that's how you know they're lying. The night they're talking about was the night Tina shot me in the leg. I was at the hospital."

Diana couldn't help but chuckle. "Sounds just like her," she muttered. Then, she stood up and walked around the table to where Ray Ray sat. She placed a stack of photographs onto the table, standing behind him as she did so.

"So, Who's this?" Diana asked, her voice calm but firm.

Ray Ray leaned forward, catching a whiff of her perfume, and for a split second, his eyes softened, but he quickly composed himself. "That ain't me. Might look like me from behind, but most brown-skinned, 5'10" brothers look alike from behind."

Diana raised an eyebrow but pressed on. "So, where were you that night again?"

Ray Ray leaned back in his chair, arms crossed, his gaze never leaving hers. "I just told I was in the hospital."

Diana wasn't convinced. "Do you have proof?"

Ray Ray paused, then shook his head. "No, I didn't take pictures because I was injured. But hold up…" He reached into his pocket and pulled out his phone to show the hospital bill. "Here's the bill they gave me."

Diana took the phone, looking at the bill her eyes scanning the details. She noticed the date and time lined up perfectly with the timeline of the alleged crime. "Well, there you go," she said, her tone softening a little.

Ray Ray leaned forward, a small grin tugging at his lips. "See, I told you."

Diana sighed, her expression turning more serious. "Still, I really need you to start cleaning up your life, because they are going to try to find something to pin. They don't like to be embarrassed."

Ray Ray met her gaze, lingering on the scent of her perfume that still lingered in the air. "I'll do whatever you ask me to do Di," he said, his voice quiet but sincere.

Diana made a face, walking around the table to stand on the other side, keeping her distance. Ray Ray's eyes followed her movements, appreciating the way she carried herself and the way her curves flattered her petite body.

"Instead of going by Ray Ray," Diana said, crossing her arms, "I need you to start going by Raynard."

Ray Ray leaned back in his chair, his expression shifting to a more defiant one. "Man, I don't even look like a Raynard. That name is foreign to me."

Diana gave him a firm, encouraging look. "Well, that's your name, and that's how we change the narrative. By showing that you're an upstanding black man who would never do what they're accusing you of."

Ray Ray hesitated, then nodded slowly. "Alright, I'll go with it."

Diana nodded in approval. "Good. I'll see you later. I've got to get ready to head out."

Ray Ray stood up, still looking at her with a hint of curiosity. "Oh, your man ready to go out this early?"

Diana laughed softly, the sound light and easy. "I don't have a man, unfortunately."

Ray Ray raised an eyebrow. "Oh, word? A good fine woman like you?"

Diana gave a small, knowing smile. "That doesn't have anything to do with being a good woman. Men aren't looking for a good woman."

Ray Ray chuckled, shaking his head. "That's a lie, I'm working on being a better man. Hopefully, you can help me with that."

Diana gave him a nod of acknowledgment as Ray Ray walked out the door.

Diana grabbed her bag, she begins to drive over to Mya's house, her mind kept drifting back to Ray Ray. The way he'd looked at her, the way his words lingered in the air. She couldn't deny the chemistry between them, the way he tried to flirt, his charm that seemed effortless. She quickly snapped herself out of it. No, she thought, shaking her head. That's my best friend's baby daddy. I can't let anything happen between us. Not like that.

Her hands gripped the steering wheel a little tighter as the thought lingered.

The silence in the car was deafening as she drove, and the longer she thought about Ray Ray, the more she realized how much she missed having someone in her life. Someone who wasn't wrapped up in the complications of everyone else's mess. She quickly reminded herself of the truth she knew deep down.

Diana pulled up to Mya's house, her eyes catching sight of Trevor across the street, standing with a girl Diana didn't recognize. For a moment, her chest tightened. It's fine, she told herself. It's been a while. Although seeing him with someone else, especially after everything that had happened between them, still stung. It was how she and Mya had met—through Trevor, and though it had led to their strong friendship, it didn't make it any easier to see him moving on.

Trying not to acknowledge the knot forming in her stomach, Diana quickly looked away and got out of the car. She shook off the feeling and made her way to the front door. She knocked, hoping the distraction of seeing Mya would help her forget the ache.

James opened the door, and Diana's eyes widened in surprise. The last time she had seen him was at church.

"Is Mya here?" Diana asked, trying to mask her confusion.

James nodded, stepping aside. "Yeah, come on in. I'll get her. You can sit on the couch."

Diana entered, still trying to process the situation. She made her way to the couch, watching James walked away, wondering just how much had changed. Her thoughts were interrupted when Mya walked out, looking surprised but happy to see her.

"Hey, girl! Come in here," Mya said, motioning for Diana to follow her into the room.

Diana stepped into the room, turning to Mya, "Who are these kids? What's going on?"

Mya chuckled, shaking her head. "Girl, calm down. These are the kids I was telling you about. The ones I was going to adopt after my party blew up." She paused, her expression softening. "Instead of letting them go back to the system, I let them stay with me."

Diana blinked in surprise, her heart swelling. "Oh my God, girl! What in the world?"

Mya nodded, a proud smile tugging at her lips. "Yeah, girl so much has been going on, but they really are great kids."

"That's good, girl, I just can't believe you adopted two kids" Diana said.

Mya sighed heavily, rubbing her temples before propping herself up on her hand. "Girl, what am I going to do about my store?"

Diana leaned forward, her tone turning business-like. "Well, honestly, she doesn't have legal authority to take your store, but Carter will. Since he didn't sign a prenup, he can fight for it. He has a pretty strong case."

Mya winced, the weight of it all settling in. "What's the best way to protect it?"

Diana's brow furrowed as she thought about the complexities of marriage law. "Marriage is a tricky thing when it comes to assets. It's like trying to say half of my body gets nutrients, but the other half doesn't. You can't separate the two once they become one."

Mya sighed again, frustration and exhaustion evident in the slump of her shoulders. "I get that," she muttered, her voice barely above a whisper. "But I did give him a prenup when I was in New York. It was after the marriage, though."

Diana's interest piqued. "Well, give it to me. I'll take a look and see what we can do, but there isn't much that can be done."

Mya nodded, then stood up to grab the paperwork from a nearby box. Diana watched her, tapping her fingers on the arm of the couch. When Mya returned, Diana couldn't help but drop a bombshell.

"So, girl, guess who I'm helping?" Diana asked, her tone playful, but there was an edge of seriousness behind it.

Mya paused, her attention shifting back to Diana as she looked through the box. "Who, girl?"

Diana smirked. "Ray Ray."

Mya froze mid-motion. Her head snapped up to meet Diana's eyes, disbelief written all over her face. "Gurrrrrllll, what?! Why?"

Diana hesitated for a moment, her expression neutral. "I can't say too much. It's a legal situation, but he is actually innocent."

Mya shook her head, her expression a mix of concern and exasperation. "Aw, poor Ray Ray. He's always in something."

Diana nodded, a bit more seriously now. "Yeah, but you know, he really isn't that bad of a guy."

Mya raised an eyebrow, her gaze sharp. "Yeah, but he cheated and dogged Tina out. She didn't deserve that."

Diana fell silent for a moment, doing her best to ignore the familiar twinge of guilt and conflict inside. She nodded slightly, her voice quiet. "I know, but people can change."

Mya watched Diana for a moment, her eyes narrowing as if she were reading her. Then, she leaned back against the couch, shaking her head. "I guess we'll see."

Chapter 24
Things, Things, Things

Mya and Diana sat on the couch in her room, catching up on everything that had been happening in their lives

Just as Diana was finishing up a story about a case she was working on, Mya's phone rang. She glanced at the screen, her heart sinking when she saw the name. London.

"Hey, Lon," Mya answered, trying to keep her voice steady.

London's voice came through the phone, slightly impatient, but also laced with concern. "Girl, what's going on at the store?"

Mya paused. She had completely forgotten to tell London about the closure. "Oh my God, I'm so sorry, I thought I told you," Mya responded, running a hand through her hair. "The store shut down because of this mess with Carter girl."

London's voice grew more concerned. "Wait, what do you mean shut down? Are you okay?" There was a brief silence as London likely scanned her surroundings, her mind working through all the questions that must've been racing through her head.

Mya sighed. "Girl, I'm fine. It's just… a lot right now. I didn't mean for you to be the last one to know."

London let out a frustrated breath. "Why am I always the last to know, though?" she asked, her voice a mix of irritation and care. "I'm over here just finding out now, I came all the way down south with you. You should've called me earlier I thought we were in this together Mya."

"I'm so sorry," Mya said, her voice softening. "There's been so much going on, and I put so much pressure on you, I didn't even think to tell you. I honestly didn't want to bother you."

There was a pause, and then London sighed again, a little more gently this time. "Okay, okay. Well, we need to discuss next steps so I can know what I need to do."

Mya smiled, grateful for London's understanding, even if she was frustrated. "Can you meet me at this Mexican restaurant? I will text you the details."

London gave a little pause, and then said, "Yeah just text me the info".

"Thank you, Lon," Mya hangs up and says 'Come on, Diana, you're coming with me." Mya shot a glance at her friend, trying to hide the playful smirk forming on her lips.

Diana raised an eyebrow, not quite sure what Mya meant. "Girl, I don't know. Tina's not here, so it's just gonna be you and me."

Mya was already standing up, heading toward the kids' room to make sure they were okay before she left. "Girl, please! You know I need you to come with me. I want to integrate London with us."

Diana shook her head, "Alright, alright. But don't expect me to be all buddy-buddy with her, okay?"

Mya laughed, a lightness in her chest as she glanced over her shoulder. "Just come, girl."

Diana quickly texted Tina: "On my way to get you.

We're going to the Mexican spot. Meet me outside!" As she hit send, she turned her attention to Mya, who was in the middle of getting ready to leave.

Mya was making sure everything was in order, looking back at the kids. "Alright, y'all, I'll be back soon."

As she stepped outside, Trevor came jogging across the street, his eyes landing on Mya with a casual but curious expression.

"Hey, bro," Mya greeted, leaning against the car as she waited for him to catch up.

"What's good? What's D doing over here?" Trevor asked, glancing toward the house, his eyebrows raised.

Mya chuckled, shaking her head. "She's my best friend, Trev. You know that."

"I know, I know," Trevor responded, still looking over at the house. "I just haven't really seen her around until you came back."

Mya nodded, understanding what he meant. "She came by to help me with some legal stuff," she explained.

Trevor turned slightly, his expression becoming more casual, though his tone hinted at something else. "Oh, okay, cool. She still looking good, man."

Mya folded her arms across her chest, a teasing smile tugging at her lips. "Oh no, Trev. You are my brother and all, but you are not about to break her again with all your side pieces."

Trevor chuckled, but there was a shift in his expression as he shrugged. "Nah, it wasn't like that. She was going her way, and I was going mine."

Mya gave him a pointed look, her arms still folded. "Your way was going to prison and cheating."

Trevor sighed, the familiar frustration creeping back into his voice. "Here you go again, Mya. I did my time. I'm working now, and I'm good." Trevor looked at her, his tone shifting as he asked, "Where you going?"

Mya shrugged, tossing him a quick glance. "Out with my friends."

DIANA

Diana pulled up to Tina's house, the engine purring as she parked the car. Tina was standing outside, chatting on her phone, her hands animated as she gestured in the air.

Tina hung up the phone with a quick, "I'll call you when I get back," before slipping the phone into her purse and walking toward the car.

As she got in, Diana greeted her with a playful grin. "That must was Chase?"

Tina rolled her eyes and grinned mischievously. "Oooo, you nosey."

"And is," Diana said with a chuckle.

Tina hesitated for a moment, then relaxed back into the seat. "That was Chase."

Diana raised an eyebrow, looking over at Tina in surprise. "Oh, so y'all getting close, huh?"

Tina's smile softened as she nodded. "Yeah, actually, we are. I wasn't expecting it, but I'm glad it did. It feels really good."

"That's great, girl," Diana replied, her tone warm. "You deserve some love and happiness."

Tina sighed, a smile lingering on her lips. "I'm so done with Ray Ray. Anybody can have him at this point. Chase is different. He communicates with me, he's helping me get my business off the ground, and he just... he makes me feel good. He's been teaching me, supporting me, and loving me. He's just so nice."

Diana raised her hands in mock surrender. "Hold up. I know you ain't falling in love over the phone."

Tina laughed, shaking her head. "Girl, no. But I'm going to New York tomorrow to see him. Spend some time with him."

Diana nearly slammed on the brakes at the sudden information. "What?! Without me? You better not be staying in his house"

Tina busts out laughing. "Girl, he wants to show me around his town. Just get to know me better. And nope he got me a room."

Diana was still in shock. "Girl, don't be out there having sex with that man."

Tina shot her a look of disbelief. "I'm not you need to acting like the Virgin Mary, but I'm going to wait a little longer."

Diana raised an eyebrow, her voice dropping to a teasing tone. "How about... you wait till marriage?"

Tina snorted. "I'm not there yet, girl."

Diana dramatically sighed, shaking her head. "Jesus."

Just then, they pulled into the parking lot of the restaurant. Diana parked, and they got out of the car, making their way inside. As they walked in, Diana spotted Mya and London already seated at a table, chatting and laughing.

Tina glanced over at them and raised an eyebrow. "What is she doing here?"

Diana gave her a pleading look, shaking her head slightly. "Please, Tina. Be nice. She wants to integrate her into the group. Let's give her a chance."

Tina sighed but nodded, looking like she was trying her best to be open. "Alright, girl. I'll try."

They walked over to the table, and Mya and London looked up, smiling as they saw them approach.

The group sat down, settling into the cozy atmosphere of the restaurant. The air was filled with the smell of fresh chips and salsa, and the soft hum of Latin music added a lively touch to the setting. The waitstaff quickly brought over water for everyone, and they all sipped their drinks while chatting.

Tina's phone buzzed, and she glanced down at the screen. Mya leaned over; her curiosity piqued. "Oooo, how's that going?" she asked with a teasing smile.

Tina quickly shifted her eyes to London before responding. "Uh, it's going good," she said, her tone almost distracted, not wanting London all in her business.

Just as they were about to dive deeper into conversation, the door to the restaurant swung open, and Damon walked in. Diana spotted him immediately. "Look who it is!" she said with a playful grin.

Mya laughed, shaking her head. "Hush, girl."

Damon approached the table with his signature grin. "Hello, ladies," he greeted, his voice warm and inviting.

"Heey," the group chorused in return.

Damon leaned against the table and raised an eyebrow, giving Mya a teasing look. "I'm always seeing you in restaurants. When are you going to let me take you to one?"

Mya chuckled, shaking her head. "Maybe if I actually get divorced."

Damon smirked. "I hear that. I'm not trying to step into anybody's covenant."

As the conversation continued, Carter appeared in the back, working, and noticed Damon chatting with Mya. He paused, his gaze narrowing as he walked over.

Tina, noticing the tension, raised her brows. "What in the world? Now this is some good lunch."

Carter stepped up to their table, looking at Damon with a half-smile. "What's good, y'all?"

Damon responded with a cool nod, "What's good, Carter? I'll holla at you, Mya."

Tina teased, "Look who got a job."

Carter shot her a quick glare. "Hush big mouth."

Mya, taken off guard, looked up at him. "What are you doing here?"

"I started a business," Carter replied, a touch of pride in his voice. "The pastor got me a gig here, painting."

Mya blinked, surprised. The thought that he was finally working hit her, but a swirl of conflicting emotions followed. Why couldn't he do this when we were together? she wondered.

"Oh Okay, that's good," she said, her voice quieter now as she turned forward, her thoughts swirling.

Carter stood there for a moment, sensing the change in her tone. Feeling dismissed, he muttered, "Alright, then. Cool." He walked away, heading back to work.

Diana, trying to break the tension, leaned back in her chair. "Oh my God, what are the odds we'd come into this place today? Your husband and your love interest all in the same spot"

A smile creeping across Tina face. "That was God's work right there."

Diana rolled her eyes playfully. "Oh hush, don't start."

Mya, still processing everything that had just happened, looked ahead. "I don't know what that was, but that right there was awkward."

London spoke up with a smile. "Well, I'm glad you stood your ground."

The group laughed, the mood lightening once again as they enjoyed their food. They stayed at the table a while longer, catching up and chatting about everything and nothing. After a while, they paid the bill and stood to leave.

As Mya walked toward the door, she glanced over her shoulder. Carter was back to work, his focus now solely on painting the walls. She watched him for a moment, still feeling the sting of the past, but also a strange warmth in her chest. Even though she's hurt and angry, it feels good to see him working, she thought. He's doing well, and I want the best for him, even if we're no longer together.

Chapter 25
Carter

Carter wiped the last of the paint off his hands as he finished the final touches on the patio. The job was done, and he felt a small sense of pride in the work. He walked toward Hernandez, who was standing outside the house, waiting for him.

"How much?" Hernandez asked, his voice gruff.

Carter cleared his throat, eyeing the work he'd done. "Well, I painted the whole back and the patio. It'll be $700."

Hernandez pulling out his wallet and handing Carter a check. "Here you go, Thank you Carter."

Carter took the check, offering a nod. "God bless," he said, his voice sincere as he turned to load his tools into the back of his truck.

As he packed up and was walking out the door, he noticed Damon walking toward him. Carter's first instinct was to keep moving, not wanting to deal with any tension, but Damon called out to him.

"Hey, Carter man, hold up," Damon said, stepping into his path. "Look, I know what that looked like and I wasn't trying to make a pass at your wife. We've just known each other a long time, that's all. I respect you, man."

Carter could hear the words, but something in his gut told him Damon was lying. He thought about throwing some sarcastic remark back, but instead he just nodded.

"I hear you, man, thank you for letting me know" Carter said, his voice neutral. "I know you know what's going on, but that's still my wife and I'll be back with her soon."

Damon met his gaze, nodding with a small smile. "That's good man. I'll see you around."

Carter watched as Damon turned and walked away, heading toward his nice truck. Carter's eyes lingered on the truck for a second, his jaw tightening, before he turned and walked toward his beat-up pickup. He slammed the door with a thud, the sound echoing in the quiet air. The truck was old—too old, and it creaked as he cranked it up, the engine sputtering to life with a loud cough.

Carter's knuckles gripped the steering wheel as he pulled out of the driveway, heading toward his house. The engine roared, struggling to keep up with the speed. But before he reached home, he took a sharp turn and drove toward Jamal house.

Carter pulled up to Jamal's house, the tires of his old truck grinding against the gravel as he parked. Jamal was outside, grabbing the mail, and Carter got out to join him.

"I see why my daddy always got his own mail," Jamal said with a grin, flipping through the envelopes. "Feels good, feel like you own something in this world."

Carter chuckled, shaking his head. "Man, you old."

Jamal gave him a side-eye. "How'd your first day go, bro?"

"It went really good," Carter said, stretching his neck. "Took all day, but it was quick money."

Jamal gave him a playful smirk. "Quick money huh – How's it feel to finally make your own money?"

Carter laughed dryly. "Don't start, man. I didn't just sit around on purpose. The injury kept me from working before."

Jamal raised an eyebrow. "Yeah, that's what you say. Injury put you down for some years ten to be exact"

They walked toward the house, Carter following Jamal inside. Jamal grabbed a cold bottle of water and tossed it to Carter.

"So, where's Nancy?" Carter asked, taking a sip.

Jamal waved a hand dismissively. "She's out helping her mama with something."

Carter shrugged. "I knew she wasn't here because the house too quiet."

Jamal settled on the couch, and Carter plopped down beside him. "Man, I saw Mya at the restaurant today. I was painting at the spot, and she was there with her friends or whatever."

Jamal's eyes narrowed. "Oh yeah? How'd that go?"

Carter's voice dropped, frustration creeping in. "Damon popped up, trying to hit on her."

Jamal blinked, glancing over at Carter. "Damon? Lil dude from high school? Well, ain't she single now?"

Carter clenched his jaw. "No. We're still married. We're fighting for it, man. Well, I'm fighting for her."

Jamal nodded slowly, understanding the weight behind Carter's words. "I don't blame you for that, bro. So, what'd you do?"

Carter's gaze darkened. "I walked over there. She was shocked to see me working, man."

Jamal cut in, laughing a little. "I was shocked you were working."

Carter shot him a look. "That's messed up, man."

"My bad, bro," Jamal said with a quick grin, but then his face turned serious. "But what'd you do after that?"

Carter's shoulders sagged as he rubbed his forehead. "I approached them, but she didn't acknowledge me, so I just went back to working. I don't know, man. I just can't think about her being with another man. I know I messed up. I shouldn't have done half the things I did but name a man who hasn't."

Jamal leaned back, tapping his fingers on the armrest. "I haven't."

Carter blinked, the surprise clear in his eyes. "Everybody not perfect like you then I guess."

Jamal held his ground. "Nah I'm not saying that, but you can't use your mistakes as an excuse to get her back, bro."

Carter exhaled sharply. "I know, I know, But we've been together since high school, man. It's hard to just let it all go."

Jamal's voice softened, but his words were firm. "I know, bro. Maybe she wants to see what else is out there."

Carter's chest tightened. "There's nothing else out there. All she need is me."

Jamal shrugged. "Alright, King Kong, calm down. You went and saw what was out there. The only difference is she might upgrade from you and that's why you're scared" he said with a playful grin. "Let's just play the game."

Carter gave him a half-hearted smile as Jamal booted up the game system, but his mind was elsewhere.

Chapter 26
Tina

Tina got home later that evening. She waved goodbye to Diana, who was heading out, and stepped into her apartment, thankful to have it to herself. Her kids were over at her mama's house, and she finally had some peace and quiet.

With a heavy sigh, she made her way to her room, intending to pack her bag for her upcoming trip to New York. The idea of spending time with Chase and starting a new chapter was exciting.

Suddenly, a sharp knock at the door startled her. Tina froze for a moment "Who could that be banging on my door." She slowly approached the door and opened it, only to find two police officers standing on the other side.

Her pulse quickened as she tried to keep her composure. "Ray Ray isn't here," she said quickly.

One of the officers spoke calmly, his voice stern but professional. "We're looking for Tina Watson."

Tina's stomach dropped. "That's me," she said, her voice shaky.

"We have a warrant for your arrest," the officer continued, handing her a piece of paper.

Tina's heart raced as she tried to make sense of what was happening. "For what?" she demanded, panic rising in her chest.

The officer gave her a look of sympathy, though it didn't soften his tone. "You'll have to talk to the judge about that."

Before she could say anything else, they stepped forward and placed her in handcuffs. The reality of the situation hit her all at once. Tina was arrested. She couldn't wrap her mind around it.

As they led her to the car, her thoughts were consumed with worry. What did Ray Ray do now? she thought, feeling the weight of the unknown press down on her. She wasn't sure what she'd be walking into, but she feared the worst.

Once at the station, Tina was escorted into the holding area. Her nerves were on edge, her stomach in knots. This wasn't supposed to be happening. She was supposed to be going to New York in the morning, spending time with Chase, finally letting herself enjoy life again. But now... she didn't know when or how this nightmare would end.

After a few moments, she was allowed to make a call. The officer handed her the phone, and Tina dialed Diana's number, hoping Diana could somehow make sense of everything.

The phone rang twice before Diana picked up.

"Girl, this me, Tina," she said quickly, her voice trembling.

Diana's voice was full of concern. "Girl, what are you doing there?"

"I don't know Girl. If I did, I would've started with that. It's probably something Ray Ray did" Tina said, nearly breaking down. "Please, come get me girl. I'm not made for this."

Diana was quick to respond. "I'll make some calls, don't say nothing to nobody."

Tina tried to say something more, but before she could get another word out, the call abruptly ended.

Her heart sank as she lowered the phone, unsure of what was going to happen next. The officer motioned for her to follow him, and she walked back to the cell with a sinking feeling in her chest.

Sitting down on the hard bench, she was scared, confused, and above all, worried about her kids. They needed her, and she was stuck here not knowing what was going to happen next.

Just when things seemed to be turning around with Chase, this happened. She couldn't understand why it had to be now. She wasn't sure how long she'd be stuck here, but all she could do was hope Diana would come through for her.

DIANA

Diana hung up the phone with Tina, her heart pounding in her chest

The phone rang once before Mya picked up. "Hey girl" Mya answered, calmly.

"Girl how about Tina just got arrested," Diana said quickly, the words tumbling out.

Mya's voice was sharp with concern. "What? Why?!" she demanded.

"I don't know yet, but I'm gonna find out. I just wanted to let you know," Diana replied, trying to steady herself.

Mya paused for a moment clearly processing the news. "Okay, keep me updated, Diana. I'm here if she needs me."

Diana nodded, even though Mya couldn't see her. "I will, I promise."

She ended the call, her mind racing. Tina in trouble was the last thing she expected to hear. Diana quickly reached out to a few people she knew who could help get Tina out on bail. She didn't hesitate. Not for a second.

After a few hours of back-and-forth calls, arrangements were made. Diana couldn't breathe easy until she knew Tina was free. The moment she got the call that Tina had been released, Diana rushed to the station.

When Tina emerged, looking disheveled and drained, Diana wasted no time. She rushed over and enveloped Tina in a tight hug. "Girl, are you okay?" Diana asked, her voice soft but full of concern.

Tina nodded, though the exhaustion was evident on her face. "I am now, that was the scariest place I've ever been in my life" she muttered, stepping back and getting into the car. Diana slid into the driver's seat and started the engine.

As they pulled away, Tina sighed deeply. "What happened, Diana? Why was I arrested?"

Diana glanced at Tina, then back at the road. "It's because of what happened with Ray Ray," she said quietly. "Someone saw you shoot him in the leg and reported it."

Tina let out a shocked laugh, disbelief coloring her voice. "Are you serious? Wow, of all the things... really?" Diana's grip tightened on the steering wheel as she tried to keep her own emotions in check. "Yeah. I called Ray Ray, and he said he doesn't want to press charges against you."

Tina's eyes widened, her anger flaring up. "He better not! After everything I've done for him, he better not press charges. This is crazy. The fate of my life in his hands."

Diana turned onto the street, trying to keep her voice calm. "Girl, you need to calm down. Don't let these men get to you. They're not worth it. Pulling out guns shooting them isn't worth it at all." She glanced over at Tina, who was fuming but nodding along.

"I know," Tina said quietly. "That's one of the reasons I'm done with Ray Ray I'm not trying to get caught up in that life or any of those situations anymore."

Diana pulled into the parking lot outside Tina's apartment, the car coming to a gentle stop. She turned off the engine and looked over at Tina. "Good, because it's not worth it. I'm just glad it was something I could fix quick."

Tina gave a small smile, her exhaustion catching up with her. "I hear you. I'll keep it together. Thanks for having my back, Di."

Diana smiled softly. "Always do and always will."

Tina nodded and opened the car door. As she stepped out, Diana watched her walk toward her apartment.

Chapter 27
Diana

As Diana drove back home she picked up her phone and called Mya, needing someone to vent to. Mya picked up on the first ring. "Girl, what's up? Tina, okay?"

Diana didn't waste any time. "Girl, do you know when Tina caught Ray Ray cheating, and she shot him in the leg? Somebody saw it and reported it!"

Mya's voice went silent for a moment, then she gasped, "Girl, are you serious? I thought we were past all that. Tina has been doing that mess since forever though."

Diana sighed, her frustration evident. "I know, Mya. It's ridiculous. Tina's too pretty for that. She deserves so much more."

Mya hummed in agreement. "Exactly! Here she is, getting caught up in the same cycle, but we can't force anybody to know their worth that's something she is going to have to see on her own."

Diana was quiet for a moment before she continued, "She leaves tomorrow for New York, to go see Chase. Full paid trip, mind you. Can you believe that?"

Mya's mouth dropped in surprise. "Wait. What? That's news to me. She's really going out there for him?"

"Yeah, and I'm happy for her. She deserves it, but she don't need to bring her mess in that" Diana said, though she couldn't completely hide the hint of jealousy in her voice. "But you know what? I just... I just pray that God sends me a man, someone I can do stuff with. I'm tired of being a saved single girl."

Mya was silent for a moment, taking in what Diana said. Then she replied softly, "Girl, I've never heard you say that before. Are you looking?"

Diana shook her head, even though Mya couldn't see her. "I'm not looking, but I do want to be found. I want that connection, that love. I want to know what it feels like to have someone by my side, you know?"

Mya laughed lightly. "Aww, girl. You gotta get out there! You can't sit around waiting forever."

Diana chuckled, but there was a hint of sadness in her laugh. "I know, girl. I need to find something, because I haven't had a man in so long, I started looking at Ray Ray!"

Mya burst out laughing. "Girl, unless you trying to be in jail, I don't think that's the way."

Diana couldn't help but laugh too. "I know that's right! No Ray Ray for me."

The two of them continued laughing, the tension in Diana's chest easing, even if just a little.

Chapter 28

Chase

Chase had spent the morning cleaning up the house, making sure everything was in order for Tina's arrival. He wanted to make a good impression, especially since she was coming all the way to New York to spend time with him. As he tidied up, he glanced at his phone, noticing he hadn't heard from Tina in a while. He decided to send her a quick text, checking in to see if everything was okay.

Minutes later, his phone buzzed with a FaceTime call. Tina's name flashed across the screen. He smiled and answered, leaning against the kitchen counter. "What's up stranger, I know you not trying to run off on me." he asked, his voice warm with laughter.

Tina's face appeared on the screen, a smile tugging at the corners of her lips. "Guess what?" she asked, her voice full of excitement.

Chase raised an eyebrow, intrigued. "What, you trying to cancel?"

Tina chuckled, though there was a slight edge to her tone. "No, How about me and my ex-baby daddy had an issue, and someone called the police!"

Chase blinked in surprise, his mind racing. *Seriously?* he thought, but he quickly pushed the thought aside. He didn't want to make any snap judgments. "Are you good?" he asked, his voice softening with concern.

Tina smiled, feeling a little warmer at his genuine question. It wasn't exactly a smooth situation, but the fact that Chase cared enough to ask about her well-being meant something. "I'm okay," she said, her expression relaxing. "Just ready to get away and get free from all of this."

Chase's smile widened, his thoughts drifting away from the chaotic situation. "Well, I'll make sure your mind is clear. I'm looking forward to spending time with you."

Tina laughed, the sound light and easy. "Okay, well, I'm about to finish packing. I'll see you tomorrow."

"See you tomorrow," Chase said, his tone warm.

As he placed his phone down, he had never been one to second guess his decisions, but something about this felt... different. He couldn't shake the thought of whether he was getting himself into something he wasn't prepared for. *Is this really what I want?* he wondered.

Then his mind shifted, he remembered the way she smiled, the way her light skin glowed in the sunlight, and how her beautiful green eyes pulled him in. *She's pretty,* he thought, feeling a twinge of admiration for her.

Chase shook his head, trying to focus. The thought of *Mya* suddenly crossed his mind. He didn't even know why it was there. He wasn't with Mya—he let the thought of them go, somehow, he felt like maybe he should check in with her. As soon as the thought arrived, he quickly dismissed it. Why would I need to check in with her? he asked himself. We're not anything. She's not here, and I'm not trying to make anything complicated.

As the noise of the city buzzed outside, Chase took a deep breath, pushing the stray thoughts from his mind. His plans were set Tina would be in New York tomorrow, and he was determined to make the most of it.

He walked out to the balcony, looking out over the city. There was a lot ahead, a lot of unknowns, but at this moment, all he wanted was to enjoy the time they would spend together.

Chase walked to his room, his thoughts racing. He sat on the edge of his bed, his phone in his hand. Maybe he should let Mya know what was going on. After all, they were still friends, and their work relationship was still intact. He didn't want to keep secrets from her, but at the same time, he didn't want to make things complicated. He decided to text her anyway.

He typed out, "What's good?" and hit send.

A few moments passed before Mya responded with a playful, "Hey stranger."

Chase couldn't help but smile at her response. He typed back, "Oh wow, I'm a stranger now? I'm not the one who up and moved."

Mya's reply came quickly. "OMG, it's not like that. I heard about you bringing my friend to New York."

Chase paused, reading her message. He had been wondering whether Mya knew.

He quickly typed, "Yeah, I wanted to show her the Big Apple."

Then, his thoughts kept running through his mind. Do I need to tell Mya everything? He licked his lip, not sure what to do. Instead of overthinking, he decided to just say it.

He typed, "How about you and y'all other friend come on up too so Tina isn't alone?"

Mya responded almost immediately, "Actually, I think that would be a good idea. I miss New York so much."

Chase sat back, staring at his phone. His thoughts were swirling. What have I gotten myself into? he thought, shaking his head. This could be a disaster, especially with how mad Tina's going to be. However, it could also be a surprise. He grinned to himself, his mind already planning. I'll still have plenty of one-on-one time with her. It's going to be okay either way.

NO LOVE LOST

2026

FOLLOW ME ON IG
@JAYLAWHITEDAVIS

*TO GOD BE THE GLORY
FOREVER AND EVER AMEN*

Made in the USA
Columbia, SC
03 June 2025

58715652R00131